DEFENDING

GAY ROMANCE COLLECTION

THE NET

DEFENDING THE NET

GAME ON SPORTS ROMANCE COLLECTION

GENEVIVE CHAMBLEE

For information, contact the publisher, Hot Tree Publishing.

www.hottreepublishing.com

Editing: Hot Tree Editing

Cover Designer: Soxsational Cover Art

Formatting: Justine Littleton

ISBN: **978-1-925853-16-2**

1

AN ASTRINGENT ODOR of aged scotch mixed with sweet tobacco hung in the air, teasing Brighton's nostrils as he and his roommate, Dylan, maneuvered a path through the rowdy crowd to a table being wiped down by a waitress in a dim corner. In the swell, bodies pressed against him. Overapplied colognes and perfumes transferred and smeared onto his sleeves as he squeezed past, leaving him smelling as if he'd been in a house of ill repute by the time he'd crossed the room.

A few feet from his destination, Brighton struck what felt like a river barge—the broad chest of Gatien Glesseau, the Civets' starting goalie, with a gorgeous blonde draped on his right and a sexy redhead on his left. The impact whooshed Brighton's breath from his lungs and sent jagged heat seeping into his bone marrow, filling him with indefinable emotions. Dylan collided with his backside. To balance, Brighton splayed his palms across the soft silk of Gatien's shirt, and his stomach flipped in a weird flutter. He squelched it as best he could and blinked to clear his murky vision from the smoke. *So much for city ordinances regarding no smoking inside public businesses.* Lifting his chin, Brighton's eyes jerked to Gatien's face.

Instant frostbite. The Viking of a man's large eyes narrowed to slits with an ethereal glow beneath thick lashes, his square jaw dusted with stubble clenched, and a crease deepened across his forehead, like a crack in a cement sidewalk. His lips formed an unmoving line, taut and peeved. Even in the diffused lighting, Brighton saw Gatien's pectorals flex and strain against the fabric and the slight lump of an Adam's apple peeking above the button-down with the sleeves folded neatly at the elbows.

"Sorry," Brighton murmured, retreating and lowering his hands. Of all the people to stumble into, within fifteen minutes of arriving, he had found the one person who happily would build a pyre beneath him.

Reaching the booth, Brighton slid across the fresh-smelling leather seat and yanked at the collar of his starched button-up tucked neatly in his creased linen trousers.

The waitress looked up, tossed her rag on a tray with the empty glasses, and smiled. "What can I get you gentlemen?"

Brighton's lips moved, but he emitted no sound.

"Whatever's on tap," Dylan interjected, tugging the hem of his skintight V-neck that rode up with his every movement. Despite the amount of pulling, the shirt refused to reach the waistband of his jeggings.

The waitress giggled. "I'm afraid you're going to have to do better than that, honey. Everything's on tap tonight. The Cats are out, and they celebrate big. It's a coach's birthday."

Dylan stole a glance at his companion. Brighton failed to respond, and Dylan turned back to the waitress. "Beer, then."

"Ale, IPA, lager, malt, Pilsner, porter, or stout?"

"Oh." Dylan considered. "What do you suggest?"

"Well, striplings such as yourselves usually appreciate an IPA."

Dylan nodded. "Sounds good."

"I'll be right back with that order." The waitress collected her tray and sauntered through the mass of party-goers toward the cylindrical bar surrounding a succession of brass faucets.

Dylan scanned the room before settling his gaze on Brighton. "This is some place, huh? Posh."

Brighton silently critiqued the room. None of the watering holes he frequented had mahogany bars with chrome trim or marble fountains. "Maybe a little too much," Brighton stated, finally finding his voice. He interlocked his fingers, his thumbs circling each other.

"Will you calm down? We're supposed to be here."

"Yeah. Right." Brighton had been reminding himself of that fact for the last forty-eight hours, but being drafted still hadn't punctured his bubble of reality. The surrealism of hearing his name announced and being handed a jersey had faded a smidgen, but not enough to allow him comfort. His dream had come true, but why?

He looked back at Gatien who still stared with a continued annoyed expression. Brighton released a shaky breath. *Relax.*

"Hey," Semien greeted, plopping down beside Brighton and brandishing a smile that could reflect light. He extended his free hand to fist-bump Brighton, then set his drink on the table. "Glad to see you made it, bruh. I was about to give up on you, and that wouldn't be a good thing."

Dylan's eyes sparkled at Semien's arrival, and he angled his head to enhance his profile. "We wouldn't miss it for the world, sugah."

"Why is that?" Brighton inquired of Semien, arching his brow at his old college chum and former teammate who he hadn't seen in close to a year.

"Well, it's kind of a thing—an unwritten rule, like an unofficial OTA—that the team socialize outside of the arena."

Brighton brows arched higher. "OTA?"

"Organized team activity."

"Oh. I doubt anyone would miss me."

Semien snorted. "Oh, they would. And then you'd be on the list."

"What list?" Dylan asked.

"One he doesn't want to be on. And you are?"

"That's right. You two haven't met. Semy, this is Dylan Winterfield, my roommate for the past two years," Brighton introduced. "Dylan, this is—"

"I know who he is," Dylan interrupted. "You're Semien Metoyèr, SLSU's record holder for the most touchdowns in a single season, two-time All-American, winner of the Hugh Cock Award, and the center for the Civets."

"Goals, and it's the Hubert Cook Award," Semien corrected. "Although, I do have a—"

"Don't say it," Brighton warned.

"Whatever. You know what I'm talking about." Dylan waved a hand in dismissal. "You're in SLSU's Who's Who Hall of Fame."

Semien leaned back against the booth and studied Dylan's slim build and short, not-a-hockey-player stature. "That would be me. But I thought athletes were required to live in the athletic dorm."

Brighton shook his head. "Not anymore. There was a stink over Bruce Hall having its own cafeteria, and new school regulations deem that unless divided by gender or marital status, all dorms must be accessible to all students. A lot changed after you left. I got transferred to Collins, where I met Dylan. After graduation, he and I got a place together. We're living over on Audubon Avenue in a townhouse. They're new, built last year. Pretty nice. We're the first people to rent our place, and it's walking distance to The Square."

Semien rolled his lips in tight. "Hmm."

Uh-oh. Brighton had seen that expression from Semien before, and it never meant anything good. However, he wouldn't question it. He already had enough stacked on his platter without adding more. "So, tell me about this list. I want to start off on the right foot."

"They don't care which foot you use as long as you show up. Just accept the drinks and pick out a karaoke selection before one's picked for you."

"But I don't—"

Semien waved his hand. "That excuse has been used by every person in this bar and hasn't worked once. Trust me. You don't want Christophe picking your music and baiting you into a duet." He nodded toward the fashionably dressed left wing who looked as if he'd been carved in marble as he conversed with teammates.

With his thumb and index finger, Dylan swiped the corners of his mouth that curved in a wicked grin. "Slay 'Em All Chris? I'll sing a duet with him any day."

Brighton lightly backhanded Dylan's bicep. "Knock it off."

"Loosen up. I'm appreciating nature."

Semien's features twisted. "First, no one calls him Chris —ever. Second, you see that two hundred and fifty pounds vault of muscle at the end of the bar?"

"Aidan Lefèvre?" Dylan ogled the statuesque forward

known to fans as the Demigod on Ice and wet his lips.

"Yeah. Dude, you mess with Christophe and you'll duet with both of Aidan's fists—the uncut, extended version. He may be a bit off-key, but he hits all his targeted notes high and low. And Nicco," Semien continued, gesturing toward the man standing beside Aidan, "will take bets on how many seconds it'll take Aidan to waylay your scrawny butt."

Brighton stiffened at the tension but was more intrigued by the men at the bar. He glanced from Aidan to Christophe and back to Aidan again. "So, it's true? I read rumors on the net and that trash news station, XJJ, but, you know, those are rumors."

"They keep it professional on the ice and in the locker room, but they're pretty open about their relationship."

"And the rest of the team is cool with that?"

"Cool with what?"

The heads of the three seated at the table snapped up to meet Christophe's smiling face.

"You and Aidan," Semien answered with a mischievous grin. "Bry finds it hard to believe that a decrypted stiff like you still have game to do anything in the bedroom."

Brighton's face drained of color, and a wave of nausea pooled at the base of his throat as the team captain looming at the table's edge gave him a sturdy once-over. Brighton straightened for the inspection, rolling his shoulders back and inhaling a constricted breath. Streams of perspiration trickled down his neck and slipped beneath his collar.

Shy of six feet, Brighton wasn't as big as most of the players, but he was swift, scrappy, and made the most of what he had to cover the net. And whatever that was had been sufficient to land him the backup goalie position. Although the ink had dried on the contracts, receiving approval from the team captain wouldn't hurt and went a long way.

"I... I...," Brighton stammered.

Christophe held up his palm and turned to Semien, his blue eyes glimmering in the fluorescent lighting and yielding an almost otherworldly luminescence. "You clean your lip prints from the john mirror where you practice your tongue action yet, junior? It's bad PR for the franchise when anyone using the crapper has to look at themselves through your smudge and slobber."

"You're not going to be able to call me junior much longer, pops, since Bry's come aboard. He's the baby now."

Brighton shook his head and wiped his palms on his thighs. "I'm older than you."

"By a year," Semien clarified.

"Twenty months," Brighton corrected.

"I meant on the team."

"Eh, don't worry," Christophe stated. "We may keep you around a little longer, greenhorn. We need a backup mascot." Before Semien could dodge, Christophe mussed his hair into a disarray of spikes and frizz.

"Oh, c'mon, not the hair," Semien complained, standing and suppressing a laugh. "You bumhole. How am I supposed to look suave for the cameras with my hair like this?"

"That wasn't going to happen anyway."

"Just because you have dandruff beneath your organic hair plugs doesn't mean you have to take it out on the rest of us."

"What the hell are organic hair plugs?" Christophe wagged his finger at Semien. "You know, you really are a special kind of stupid sometimes, like the kind of person who would spell his name with a comma in the air."

Christophe refocused on Brighton. "We have a tradition here. Did junior tell you?"

"About the karaoke? Yes, sir."

"Sir?" Christophe chuckled. "It's Christophe. 'His majestic, omnipotent god of the most supreme,' if you must." He made a grand sweep with his arms.

"More like impotent," Semien interjected, combing his fingers through his mane.

"Keep it up and I'm going to string Vadium's socks like cheap garland throughout your apartment and hot glue them to every article of clothing you own, creating an odor so foul your own mother won't acknowledge you. Now run along while the grown folks talk."

Semien grunted and then shuffled toward a group of his teammates throwing virtual darts. "I'll be back," he called over his shoulder. "Don't let him bully you into any of that old dude disco crap."

"I happen to have an exquisite taste in music."

"Now that's a full Crock-Pot of bull," Nicco stated, stepping behind Christophe.

"Nicco, no one called you," Christophe griped. "I'm handling this."

"And we all have to listen to it in high definition." Nicco swirled the liquor in his glass and leaned closer to the table. "There're over three hundred songs to choose from. Pick what you want."

Christophe shoved Nicco's shoulder. "That won't be necessary. I've chosen a grand selection for you."

Dylan wetted his lips and angled his chin as if posing for a magazine cover. "What will we be singing, Chris?"

Christophe and Nicco exchanged a fleeting glance before both averted their attention to Dylan.

"Well, my original thought was for Brighton to sing

'Macho Man.' But on second thought, maybe it should be 'Double Dutch Bus.'"

"Or 'The Hustle,'" Nicco muttered.

Brighton's armpits dampened, and he swallowed thickly. "Why 'Macho Man'?"

"Why not?" Christophe asked, returning his focus to Brighton. "You're supposed to bring muscle to the net, right?"

"Actually, I thought it was to warm the bench since Paul Mallard transferred to the Talons," Brighton replied.

Dylan snickered.

"That's funny?" Nicco inquired.

"Yeah. Brighton doesn't ride the pine. He's a starter— the best goalie there is. Unstoppable. A number four draft."

"You don't say?" Christophe uttered with a slight movement of his head that would be an injustice to call a nod. He peered at Dylan in silence for several moments before addressing Brighton. "Paul played, you know."

"He did?" Nicco asked.

Christophe elbowed Nicco in the gut. "Of course, he did."

"Mm, I must've missed that game."

"He played more than one."

"Really?"

Christophe's smile waned as he turned to Nicco and hissed, "Yes."

"Huh. Well, what do you know?" Nicco grunted. "I'll be a monkey's uncle."

"Nicco, you couldn't be an amoeba's daddy much less a higher primate's, so please don't reproduce. Now, I'm trying to have a conversation with *Brighton,* but it seems everyone wants to interrupt."

"Spare me." Nicco snorted. "He doesn't want to talk to

you. No one does. Besides, look at him. You've got him sweating like a television evangelist caught in a whorehouse on Easter with two anal plugs, a jar of deviled eggs, and petroleum jelly."

Brighton's face drained from white to ghastly gray—the shade of gray one turns when rigor mortis begins to set in.

"Will you stop talking?" Christophe snapped. "I'm not even going to ponder what kind of freakfest you got going on with deviled eggs and petroleum."

Nicco's bottom lip jutted forward. "It's not all that freaky."

The waitress brought the drinks and distributed them to Brighton and Dylan.

"I'm back," Semien announced with a wide grin, waving a fine-tooth comb like a saber. He plopped onto the leather seat and nudged Brighton's shoulder. "This old man still wagging his dentures?"

"Oh, good gawd!" Christophe griped, then gulped the remainder of his drink. Once done, he snatched the beer in front of Brighton, chugged it, set the empty glass on the table with a clink, and faced Semien. "The big kids wouldn't let you play with the sharp darts, would they?"

"It's a virtual dartboard."

"Just like your sex life." Christophe pivoted to leave but called over his shoulder to Brighton, "Poo boo, you're on in five minutes."

"He means you," Nicco explained, pointing to Brighton and following Christophe. "And his five minutes are more like three."

"Poo boo?" Brighton quipped.

"Don't worry. He nicknames everyone. Could be worse. During a game, he called Ned Freeze 'quaggy schlong,' and now his own teammates call him that. It even got picked up on the internet, and now there's a Quaggy Schlong Fan Club dedicated to Ned."

"Gads! Is there any possibility he would reconsider?"

Semien smirked. "Not in this lifetime, but you could try groveling."

"Poo boo, though," Brighton muttered.

Dylan traced the rim of his beer with his finger. "Poo boo isn't so bad. It suits you."

Frowning, Brighton shifted in his chair. "You and Christophe seem pretty tight to carry on the way you do."

"I told you, we're like family here." Semien tapped his index finger on the tabletop. "My first week of training camp, my mom's house caught on fire in the middle of the night. Christophe showed up almost the same time the fire department did. I don't know how he knew. He arranged us hotel rooms, and the next morning, there were four suitcases —one for my mom, one for me, and one for each of my sisters—with seven outfits each, one for each day of the week."

"I remember that night. It was tough on your mom. Y'all were lucky to escape without anyone being hurt. Those old houses go up like kindling."

"You know, that house was all my mom had besides us kids. I know it looked a tread above a shanty, but she worked three jobs to pay the mortgage." Semien lowered his eyes and shook his head. "Christophe did more for me and my family in one night than my sperm donor's done his entire life. That's the kind of man Christophe is. So when he asks for something, people give it to him. He's a good guy to have in your corner." He leaned back against the booth. "I can't say the same for him as a singing partner, though."

Brighton glanced back across the room to Gatien talking with his companions. The expression on the experienced goalie's face remained harsh and steely, and his eyes chilled several degrees when he caught Brighton staring.

"Does this *family* ideology go for all team members?"

"Pretty much, except for Enok. But that's only because his English isn't that great, and no one on the team speaks Swedish. He's learning, though." Semien laughed. "Christophe dragged him on stage and made him sing 'Boogie Oogie Oogie.' That was a riot. I nearly pissed my pants laughing."

"And now the greenhorn, Brighton Rabalais, is going to bring back some of that nasty disco funk singing 'Kung Fu Fighting,'" the DJ announced over the PA. "Come on up to the stage, poo boo."

"Geez!" Brighton gasped. "You weren't kidding, were you?"

"Nope."

Dylan hopped up and pulled at his sweater. "That's us," he chirped.

"I believe the intention is to have Brighton do this alone."

"Nonsense," Dylan replied, gesturing for Brighton to hurry. "Chris expects the both of us."

Semien darted a callous glower at Dylan.

"Dylan, maybe I should—" Brighton cut his statement short as Dylan flitted through the sea of people.

"Come on, Bry," he yelled above the den of laughter and voices. "They're waiting."

"Oh, heaven bless," Brighton mumbled, scooting out of the booth.

"Hey, this one is for the team, bruh." Semien gave him two thumbs up. "Make us SLSU alums proud."

"You didn't graduate."

"Small technicality." Semien raised his glass. "Cheers!"

2

"WELL, THAT WAS COMPLETELY HUMILIATING." Brighton sighed and leaned against the wall near the rear exit.

"Dude," Semien chuckled, "I thought Enok and Vadium were bad, but you...." Semien threw back his head and laughed again. "Did you get any notes right?"

"Hush up."

"You might be the person who makes Christophe rethink this whole karaoke business. What you did was priceless. I've never heard anyone suck as bad as you."

"Gee, thanks. Your unconditional support is duly noted."

Semien patted Brighton on the shoulder. "C'mon. I promised the honey at the bar I'd buy her a drink."

Brighton shook his head. "You go ahead. I'm just going to stand here a little longer and hope the bricks open into a vortex and wrench me through to the other side."

"I'd be careful what I wished for if I were you. There are probably some really mongo rats on the inside of that wall. But if you get thirsty, you know where to find me."

"Ah, don't listen to him," Dylan said once Semien was out of earshot. "We weren't all that bad."

"Not that bad?" he just short of shouted, but with the music blaring, no one noticed. "I burped into the mike on the first note and hiccupped through the remainder of the song. And look at my shirt. If I wring it, I could salt the next ocean."

"I'm sure no one noticed."

"And did you really have to twerk?"

Dylan stared down and polished his nails on his chest. "I was feeling the music. Besides, I had to add a little flavor for the audience. You were stiff as a corpse."

"Oy!"

"What are you so worried about?"

"I have to work with these people. I'd appreciate it if they didn't think of me as a joke. It's not like I don't have enough going against me as is."

"Like what?"

"Well him, for one thing." Brighton nodded toward Gatien.

"Who's that?"

"Only Gatien Glesseau... the *goalie*. The person whose job I'm scabbing."

"What do you mean scabbing? You got canker sores or something?"

Folding his arms across his chest, Brighton shifted his weight. "I'm being serious."

"So am I." Dylan slapped his hands on his hips. "What are you talking about? You were drafted by this team."

"Yeah. *This* team. What a convenient coincidence."

"You're not making any sense."

"Haven't you been listening to anything I've said in the last three weeks about the salary disputes?"

"Yeah, I listen," Dylan replied, his tone lackluster as he scanned the room.

"Then you'd know Gatien's one of the players at an impasse in contract negotiations. He could walk out. Paul Mallard already left, so he wouldn't be in a position to take over while Gatien's being fined because the owners won't pay him what he's worth and he's refusing to play in protest."

"*Pfft!* He makes plenty of money. All players do."

"And the owners make a shitload more."

"That's all politics. It has nothing to do with you."

Brighton pressed his lips together and glanced at Gatien. "You tell that to him."

Dylan bit his bottom lip for a moment before speaking again. "Are you being paid as much as he is?"

"Of course not."

"And if there were no dispute, would you have accepted the job at your current salary?"

"Yes."

"Do you think you're underpaid?"

"No."

"Then there you have it." Dylan flung his arms in the air. "If you're not complaining, why should he?"

"Because he has far more experience."

"And you're the number four draft pick."

Brighton's face scrunched in an oval of crimson wrinkles. "Will you stop saying that?"

"But it's true."

"And? It makes"—*you sound stupid*—"me look unprofessional." Brighton shook his head. "You were boasting to Christophe and Nicco like it would impress them."

"It should."

"Look around, Dylan. There are plenty of number four

drafts in this room. And while you're taking stock in numbers, both Christophe and Nicco were number one picks in their classes. Semien was a number two pick. And the man you think shouldn't complain about his salary, well, he was a number four pick, too, with way more accolades and better stats than me, not to mention three national championships. The only reason he was a number four draft was because the first three teams had good goalies but were slacking in defensemen."

"At least you're honest about what you're doing," a gruff voice to Brighton's right stated.

Dylan's eyes grew wide at the bulky goaltender before he slowly slunk into a nearby darkened corner.

"Mr. Glesseau." Brighton's spine grew rigid. *Shit!* "I didn't see you come over, and I'm not here to—"

"Save it, young buck. Your intentions are irrelevant. I know how this game is played. Instead of the owners putting veteran players out to pasture and ending their suffering quickly as any hunter humanely treats a kill, the establishment depreciates us as a commodity and claims us as a tax write-off while you whippersnappers traipse in and bleach their soiled drawers because you're so thirsty to snatch any chance you can get. But you have to start some-where. It's the cutthroat world of hockey."

Brighton's lips thinned. "Every team has a backup."

Gatien's eyes glimmered before fading to an imposing glare. "Who do you think you're talking to? I'm not stupid. Teams don't pick top drafts to warm benches. They pick for need—to fill positions and voids, or as leverage for trades to fill positions and voids." His shoulders slack, he shoved his fists in his pockets. "Welcome to the team." He pivoted and lumbered back into the thick of the partygoers.

Brighton stared after Gatien until he'd vanished from view.

"Wow," Dylan stated, returning. "He seems a barrel of giggles. That was intense."

"What did you expect?" Brighton shook his head. "I knew coming here was a bad idea." He headed toward an exit.

"Where are you going?"

"Home."

"You're going to let that guy run you off?"

He spun to face Dylan. "You don't get it. I'm hired to do a job. This right here"—he pointed to the floor—"isn't it. My job is on the ice catching pucks." He started walking again.

"Wait." Dylan grabbed Brighton's forearm and stopped him. "He's jealous, that's all."

Brighton snatched his arm away. "No, Dylan, he wants to be treated fairly."

A hand patted Brighton on the back, and he turned in time to see Christophe passing with a sympathetic smile and wink. Aidan trailed Christophe with an equal expression of commiseration.

"Great." Brighton threw up his hands. "Now I look like some pathetic sap."

"You can't leave," Dylan protested. "The band hasn't performed. Besides, Semien said we're family."

"You stay and mingle with the cousins, then. I have to get out of here. I need air." Not waiting for a response from Dylan, Brighton zigzagged through the mob to a side exit and slid outside into the alley.

The stench of raw sewage, rotting food, and decaying rodents rose from the pavement and wafted from the dumpsters. Covering his nose and mouth with his forearm, Brighton meandered to the front of the building, waited for a streetcar to pass, crossed the street onto the neutral ground —the grassy area between the streets—and leaned against a gas streetlamp. There, the air was humid but void of odor, as if the stench knew not to leave the alleyway. Muffled hums of jazz, swamp rock, blues, and zydeco floated from the various businesses lining the streets.

Not many tourists roamed this part of the city, as locals tended to guard admission with passwords, codes, and secret entrances into the town's most treasured establishments—traditions handed down from previous generations of Saint Anne's affluent society.

He watched as another streetcar went past. What he should've been doing was hopping on one and heading home. With Dylan gone, it would be quiet, and he could... what? Be alone with his thoughts? Presently, his thoughts didn't like him. Or maybe he didn't like his thoughts. Either way, spending the evening with them promised to be as pleasant as consuming a half bottle of Syrup of Black Draught.

He needed a distraction.

Rolling his gaze upward, he studied the fluttering moths and fireflies dancing waltzes, tangos, and rhumbas in the gentle streams of light. Maybe instead of venturing into hockey, he should've focused on entomology. He shared a common element with the field, feeling like he'd been autopsied and tacked to some board for observation. Gatien had been correct in that regard—they were all expendable commodities. Gatien. His round inquisitive eyes. Neatly trimmed hair. Pissy, condescending disposition. And there went Brighton's mind thinking again.

He ground his heel in the grass. *Dammit, I deserve to be here. Don't I?* Sure, he'd worked for it, but that didn't mean he'd earned it. *Damn Mike.*

"Hey!" Semien called, trotting across the street. "I thought I saw you bail."

"Yeah, it's not a good night for me, Semy."

"Is this about Gatien? 'Cause if it is—"

"It's cool. Really." *Liar, liar, pants on fire.* "I have a monster headache is all."

"It's no wonder with that piece of arsenic acid you have as a plus one. Where'd you unearth him?"

Brighton smiled—at least he hoped. "Dylan's not so bad. He's actually okay once you get to know him."

Semien snorted. "Are you kidding? That dude is a douche looking for... I don't know what he's looking for, but whatever it is, he's doing it at your expense."

"He means no harm. Things haven't been easy for him."

"Has it for any of us? Doesn't mean you have to save the world."

"I'm not trying to save the world. Hell, I can't even save myself."

"Well, you living with him is definitely self-destructive behavior." Semien arched his brow. "He is *just* a roommate, right?"

"Of course. Nothing's changed. At least not that."

"Hmm. Maybe it should."

"And maybe you should stop trying to babysit me and get back to the party. That blonde looked pretty into you."

"And now that I'm out here, she's probably into Nicco or Ramsey or whoever else's cologne she sniffed. I'm concerned about you. We've been friends a long time."

"Yes, we have, which is why you should know there's no reason for concern. I'm fine."

"You're not, but I'll drop it... for now."

"I'm going to head home. Tell Dylan for me, will you?"

Semien shook his head. "No way. That dude is on his

own. If you leave him, he's likely to get his head bashed in, and that'll be fun to watch. Let him piss off Aidan and game on. He might pull that crap with Christophe, but the Yank isn't going to have any of it."

Brighton looked at the front doors of the bar, chewed the inside of his jaw, and sighed. "I really don't feel like going back in there."

"It's a private party. Well, semiprivate. Anyway, he came as your guest. He should have the good sense to know that once you bounced, he should have, too."

Brighton pressed his palms together in a praying motion. "Please do this favor for me. I'll owe you."

"How about this? I'll tell the bouncer to be extra gentle when he tosses him out on his butt. I wonder how far he'll fly. He can't weigh more than 120 pounds. What do you think? Ten feet?"

"You're such a gentleman." Brighton tossed up his hand as he began trekking the short distance to the streetcar stop at the corner. "I'll call you tomorrow."

When the car arrived, he settled on a mahogany seat near the rear, stretching his legs in front of him and crossing them at the ankles. Brighton always found something relaxing about staring out the open window at the picturesque tree-lined boulevards veiling stately mansions, placid waterways, and sculpted gardens that led to his neighborhood of old Creole architecture. The bungalow he shared with Dylan wasn't much, but it was sufficient for two single guys with no active social life. Brighton knew why his was stagnant, but he couldn't figure out the issue with Dylan's. But tonight wasn't the time to play inspector. He actually was developing a headache.

He leaned his head back against a brass rail and screwed his eyes shut to block the carroty glow from the exposed lightbulbs overhead. An image of Gatien's inscrutable gaze dauntingly materialized. Hazel. His eyes were hazel with golden twinkles and a glint of determination that caused something to thrum through Brighton's extremities and pulsate low in his thighs. They sparkled like jewels. He'd gotten that close, that even in poor lighting Brighton had gotten a good long look. Rolling his lips inward, Brighton bit down on them, picturing Gatien's— smooth like porcelain. Full and ripe.

Why was he thinking about Gatien's eyes and lips to the verge of fantasy and odd body parts stirring?

Brighton's eyes flew open, and the world flitted into focus. His gaze darted to the lush grounds of an opulent cemetery the streetcar passed, thinking he could definitely engage in a series of impish adventures in there with Gatien if circumstances were different. If there were no salary disputes. If Brighton was an established player instead of a rookie. If Gatien wasn't his teammate. If Gatien didn't despise his presence. If Gatien liked guys.

Brighton could stop right there playing the 'if' game, considering that last one was a deal breaker.

His cell rang, pulling him from his thoughts. Withdrawing the phone, he read the screen and frowned at the name: Mike. He declined the call, stuffed the phone into his pocket, and refocused on reality.

Ah, hell!

He'd missed his stop.

3

BRIGHTON EXITED the streetcar at a sidewalk café that had seemed random when he decided on deboarding but made more sense once his stomach grumbled at the aroma of the grilling meat and sugary delights. He didn't feel hungry—in fact, he hadn't had much of an appetite all day—but the alien sounds erupting from his gut indicated otherwise.

He seated himself at an empty table and removed the menu stuck between the ketchup and mustard bottles. The problem with reading a menu when hungry was that everything looked appealing. He scanned the offerings, and concluded since it was getting late, he should stick with something light yet fulfilling. Sleeping had been an issue of late, both falling and staying, sometimes accompanied by night terrors. A doctor had prescribed pills, which Brighton allowed to collect in the medicine cabinet. He'd had enough of pills and doctors and... everything.

"Try the oyster po'boy with the chipotle mignonette sauce," a familiar voice from an adjacent table suggested.

Brighton turned and met the hazel eyes that had been

taunting him. Their heated stare tunneled beneath his skin, brushing across the nerve endings. His chest constricted. "Mr. Glesseau," he squeaked. "I didn't see you there."

"Mr. Rabalais." Gatien nodded. "You're not very observant for a goaltender, are you?" He waggled his brow. "You following me?"

Sweat beaded on Brighton's forehead. "No. Sorry. I'll go." He pushed his chair from the table and stood.

"Don't be a twit. No need to leave a public restaurant when you're obviously hungry." Gatien waited for Brighton's guttural protest to subside before motioning to the empty chair across from him. "You might as well join me if you're dining alone."

"I am, but I don't want to intrude."

"Well, it's a bit late for all of that." Gatien released a slow breath. "But there's nothing to be done about it now other than deal with it and move forward."

Brighton sat in the indicated chair, partially obscuring his face with the menu as he flipped the laminated pages with trembling fingers.

"You okay?" Gatien asked.

"Yeah. Fine." He squirmed in his chair.

Gatien folded his arms and crossed his legs. "You wouldn't admit it to me if you weren't." His expression softened. "I don't guess I blame you for that."

"Listen, Mr. Glesseau—"

"Cut the formality. That went out the window when you signed your name on the dotted line to become a Cat. About the only one who would tell you otherwise is Nicco, and that's because he enjoys any opportunity to be a first-rate ass—or a second-rate one." He shrugged. "Or just an ass in general. You'll acquire a special taste for him. We all did eventually. Didn't really have much choice. It's not like he's going anywhere anytime soon. Some guys sign on and you know it's only for a season or two. Others you know are lifers. They're either a Cat or they hang up their skates. There's no middle ground."

Brighton pushed his damp, toffee-colored waves from his eyes, noting he needed a trim. He'd been urged to have it done before Signing Day but put it off as usual. Haircuts were never on his list of favorites.

"Is that how it is for you? No middle ground?" Brighton fanned himself with the menu.

"Possibly. Are you sure you're okay?"

"Yes. It's the humidity."

"Mm." Gatien scratched his chin. He opened his mouth to speak again when the waitress arrived to take their orders.

Brighton blew out a soft sigh of relief for the interruption. "I'll have the oyster po'boy with steak fries, coleslaw, and a draft."

"Same," Gatien stated. He waited until the waitress left and then asked, "Do you want to find a table inside?"

"I'm good." *Damn this sweating.* The heat was bad, the humidity worse, and the way Gatien observed him absolutely terrifying. What was in his gaze? More than concern and ordinary curiosity. Brighton undid another button of his shirt, exposing his upper chest. Instantly he felt less constricted, and his breathing relaxed a bit. He rolled his shoulders, easing the stiffness from his muscles. "Just hot."

"You are that," Gatien mumbled.

"What?" Had Brighton heard correctly? *Did Gatien just... nah, he couldn't have. Not Gatien Glesseau. Why would he have said something like that?*

"Everything here is... fresh."

Brighton blinked. Something about Gatien's tone, the way he enunciated the sentence, had Brighton's mind flipping that Gatien had meant more than just fish. *Okay, I'm losing it. This is crazy.*

"Do you come here often?" Brighton asked. *Oh. My. God.* That sounded like a cliché pickup—and a bad one at that.

"It depends on my mood. I don't live far from here. They deliver." He grinned. "Well, to me. It helps when you know the chef and the owners."

"Oh. Did y'all grow up together?"

"Yeah, something like that." Any hardness remaining in Gatien's eyes vanished.

Sounds like a cozy relationship. Something twisted inside of Brighton in a manner that rubbed raw. He looked around the outdoor seating area. "It seems like a great little place."

"I think so. It's quality food without the formality. There's a lot to be said for simplicity." His smile lessened by millimeters. "Unlike you. You seem complex."

"Not really. I just want to play hockey."

Gatien cast a dubious gaze on him. "And that's all?"

"Yep. That's it. Sorry to disappoint you."

A period of silence ensued while Gatien appeared to ponder questions he didn't ask. Brighton couldn't imagine what, since so far Gatien had been both blunt and direct.

Finally, Gatien spoke again.

"Where's your friend?"

"He stayed at the party."

Tossing his head back, Gatien howled in laughter. "You left him with those hyenas? He must not be much of a friend. They'll pick his bones clean and use the remnants for back scratchers."

"Dylan's a big boy. He does all right for himself."

"Okay, greenhorn, here's lesson number one, something

you should've picked up on earlier tonight. The Civets are a closed group. We take care of each other and each other's family. It doesn't extend much beyond there. Your friend doesn't need to be getting any ideas that he's included in this unless you're including him." He leaned forward. "Are you?"

Brighton had an answer. However, gazing into Gatien's eyes, all thoughts evaporated. "I... I don't know," he stammered.

"Two oyster po'boys," a pretty brunette, her hair in a neat French twist and wearing an amethyst chef's coat, announced.

Gatien looked at both meals and frowned. "I ordered coleslaw, too." He nodded toward the coleslaw on Brighton's plate.

"I know," the chef said, "but I'm trying a new recipe for baked beans. I need a guinea pig. Tag, you're it."

A fondness passed between the two.

Ah, so that's what you like.

Gatien suppressed a grin and glanced at Brighton. "What was it I said about the service at this place?"

"Hush up and try it." The chef swatted Gatien's shoulder and then focused on Brighton. "I'm Gretchen." She extended her hand. "And you are?"

"Brighton," Brighton replied, shaking the petite hand.

An awareness registered on her face. "Brighton Rabalais." She nodded. "I've heard a lot about you. Gatien says you're one of the best goaltenders he's seen in a long time and that you're absolutely smoking on the ice."

"Really?"

"Yes. He's been talking about you all season—even attended some of your college games to see you play."

Gatien's mouth gaped. "Shouldn't you be in the kitchen peeling potatoes?"

"That's why I have a sous chef. And if you get ornery with me, I'll send her out here and she can peel you."

"You're such a...." Gatien scrunched his face.

Gretchen chortled. "You better not say a dirty word or I'm telling Mama."

Mama? Must be serious to have met the parental units.

Gatien unfolded his napkin and draped it across his lap. "Snitch."

"Okay, you two, enjoy your meal. I have to get back to the kitchen for my"—she glanced at Gatien—"*real* customers." She patted Brighton on the back of his wrist. "I'm not referring to you when I say that. It's nice meeting you, and if you need anything, let the staff know."

"Oh, we will," Gatien interjected.

Gretchen rolled her eyes before strolling back to the kitchen.

"She seems nice," Brighton said, having relaxed a smidgen more.

"Meh," Gatien grunted. "I suppose she is. I'm stuck with her, so I have to make the most of it."

Disappointment registered in Brighton's belly, and he dumped ketchup on his steak fries as a distraction.

Gatien smirked.

"What?" Brighton asked.

"Nothing." Gatien shrugged. "Well...," he hedged. "There are two kinds of people in the world: dunkers and drowners. Dunkers tend to want to test the waters a little at a time while drowners jump right in and cover everything." He pointed at Brighton's fries covered in ketchup. "I would've thought you to be a dunker, not a drowner."

"Why?"

"You seem cautious. Guarded. Not the type of person to rush into anything. Patient."

"Drowners aren't patient?"

"No. They can't be bothered with taking the time to dip each fry."

"And in exactly what professional journal is this theory of ketchup psychology published?"

Gatien dipped his fork in his baked beans and grinned. "Mock all you want, but it tends to be accurate."

"So, according to the ketchup theory, am I to assume from your lack of condiment application method that you're indecisive?" he asked, biting into a steak potato.

Gatien tracked the potato to Brighton's lips, watched him chew, and groaned softly when Brighton's tongue darted out to lick ketchup from his bottom lip. Brighton's eyes snapped wide with both awareness and confusion.

"No. I appreciate the potato for its natural flavor without embellishments," Gatien explained. "I don't require fancy enhancements."

What the hell is happening here? Was he getting his signals mixed? Had to be. He'd just met Gatien's girlfriend, but now it sounded like.... *I must be tired.*

Sweat rolled from the nape of Brighton's neck beneath his collar to the center of his back. "You know... I...." He tugged on his collar again. "*Whew*, it's humid tonight. I think I'm going to get this to go."

"Are you sure you should drive?"

"My car committed suicide last week. It's in for repairs. I took the streetcar, but I can walk."

"Where do you live?"

"Over on Audubon. It's not far."

Gatien brow rose. "I thought you were a local."

"I am. Well, originally I'm from Lake Charles, but I've lived in Saint Anne long enough to be considered local."

"Then you should know you're more than an hour from home on the streetcar."

"Really?" Brighton looked over his shoulder and scanned his surroundings, his jaw gaping at the recognition of his location. He knew he'd missed his stop, but he didn't realize he'd overshot by so much. *How long did I zone out on the streetcar?* "This is Corandetel Boulevard," he announced, more to himself than Gatien. "I'm in the Centre du Jardin?"

"It would seem so."

"*Coo-wee!*" His shoulders drooped. "I don't know what I was thinking."

"It's no problem. I'll give you a ride."

"No, don't trouble yourself. The streetcar is fine."

Gatien shook his head. "Listen, I'm not trying to get all up in your business yet, but it's obvious that something's going on with you."

Yet? "What do you mean yet?"

"Well, when there's something I want to know—and I'm quite sure there may be things I want to know about you—then I'll get in your business."

"And if I don't want you in my business?"

"Is that an option?" Gatien's tone was indignant.

"Yes," Brighton answered emphatically.

"How do you figure? In this age of social media and paparazzi, you have no privacy. Technically speaking, we're each a search engine away from a Big Brother investigation and drone porn footage. There's no need to get disgruntled over my mentioning it."

"If you want to know something about me," Brighton snapped, "you can ask me."

"I never said I wouldn't. But so far, you haven't been completely forthcoming."

"Then, perhaps that means it's none of your business, that it's my personal space and your intrusion is inappropriate and violating."

"And perhaps I don't accept that."

"What do you mean you don't accept it? It's my life."

Gatien hunched his broad shoulders. "And it's the internet."

"You're an ass."

"Yeah, I've been called that before. But I'm an honest ass. Other people would do it and not tell you."

"No, they wouldn't."

"You're deluding yourself if you think that."

"How would you feel if I did that to you?"

"How do I know you haven't?"

Brighton's brows shot up. "Because I haven't."

"Yet."

The sound that tumbled from Brighton's throat sounded foreign to his own ears. Either Gatien was insane or Brighton was for continuing to sit there listening to it. However, he couldn't bring himself to leave. He couldn't even bring himself to be as outraged as he should've been. Instead, he sat stupefied and plastered to his chair with his emotions ping-ponging across the emotional spectrum as he stared into those gorgeous, bewitching hazel eyes. *Dammit!*

Brighton strummed his fingers against the tabletop. "So, what do you want to know?"

"You can start by telling me why you're so tense."

"For one, you're not a big potpourri pot of aromatherapy."

Gatien lifted his arm and sniffed his armpit. "I knew I shouldn't have switched deodorants."

"Holy moly! Are you seriously smelling your pits in a public restaurant?"

"You said I stink."

"I meant your personality."

Gatien sucked in a deep breath. "Then you should've said that."

"I did."

"No. You were rambling about my odor needing therapy."

"I said... ah shit. Forget it." Brighton waved his hand in dismissal and bit into his sandwich.

"I thought you were going to get that to go."

"I changed my mind. Is that okay with you?"

Gatien smiled, and Brighton realized he'd been classically played into staying. *Smooth.*

"Look, you're hungry. I'm hungry. We have a great meal sitting before us. Let's eat, enjoy the night, and I'll give you a lift home later. Truce?"

Brighton nodded. "Truce."

4

TALKING GAVE WAY TO EATING, and Brighton devoured his po'boy faster than a slot machine spat out coins. It helped that the breading on the shellfish wasn't too thick and the oysters weren't fried to a rubbery texture. The coleslaw tanged with sweetness and crunch, while the steak fries were crispy but not oily. Brighton couldn't have requested a better meal or a more appealing presentation.

He reclined in his chair and rubbed his stomach.

"Room for dessert?" Gatien asked. "The bananas Foster is off the chain."

"I'm not a big fan of bananas."

"The bread pudding is equally yummy, and it comes with a rum sauce." Gatien shimmied at the mention of rum.

Brighton's gaze caught Gatien's and held, questioning the loopty loop he'd been tossed. In a span of a few hours, Gatien went from hostile to almost endearing—almost being the operative word. Maybe Gatien was trying to throw him off, unbalance him. But why? That didn't make sense. Gatien was already the starter and in no position of losing his job—unless, of course, he walked out. But that would be his choice and no reason to sabotage Brighton. Unless he wanted the Civets without a goaltender completely, as there was no third goalie. But Gatien didn't strike Brighton as being that kind of man. Since they'd been talking civilly, Gatien hadn't said one ill word against any players.

Brighton couldn't read him. All he could do was be mesmerized by Gatien's sensuous face—the way his eyes crinkled at the corners when he smiled, the slight dimples in his cheeks, or the nine faded freckles sprinkled across his nose that were partially obscured by his olive skin.

Gads! Brighton had counted the number of freckles. *Get a grip, man. You're completely losing it. No, you've lost it. And now I've reduced to talking to myself in second person. Shit!*

Brighton shook his head and focused on Gatien circling the rim of his beer with his fingers. *Damn, he looks good. Wait. What am I saying?* He couldn't—shouldn't—have those thoughts about a fellow teammate, especially not Gatien Glesseau, who was at least eight years his senior and had an established career, fame, and—most importantly—a serious girlfriend, perhaps fiancée. *Slow your roll—and everything else.* Of course, something in Gatien's voice indicated that he *might* like him, and that he might like other things, too. *No. Stop.* The heat began creeping up Brighton's neck again. *Shoo!*

"Huh?" Brighton asked, dragging himself out of his subconscious fog at the sound of Gatien's voice.

"Dessert?"

The waitress stood at the end of the table.

"Oh. Um... yeah. I'll have what he's having."

"I ordered the bananas Foster."

"Yeah, that'll be fine."

Gatien's mouth twisted in an ugly angle. "You just

said...." He gazed at the waitress. "Bring him the bread pudding and a black coffee—strong." He studied Brighton. "I think you need sobering up."

The waitress nodded and shuffled away.

"I'm not intoxicated."

"Well you're something, that's for sure. You're not all here."

"It's been a long night."

"What, do you go to bed at seven? It's only a little after eight."

"It feels a lot later. Guess I'm tired. Or maybe it's the heat draining me."

"Maybe." Gatien's tone sounded dubious. "It's only going to get worse when summer kicks in full swing. How have you managed living here all these years when you think this is bad?"

It was a fair question. Didn't mean Brighton intended on answering it, though. Instead, he pressed the cold beer to his cheek and inhaled. He shouldn't be staying for dessert. For one thing, the entrée stuffed him. Second, he didn't need the empty calories. Sure, he'd burn them off in little to no time, but why add them to work off?

He looked up at Gatien. *That's why.* He wanted to stay and be in Gatien's presence, which was odd because he also wanted to run as far away as possible. His emotions were insanely ridiculous. And besides all that, it was unlike Brighton to be contemplating any of these absurd musings. That was more Dylan's thing.

Dylan! Brighton had completely forgotten about his roommate. He should probably call him. And that wasn't the only thing he should probably do, but when he glanced at Gatien again, he forgot them all.

"I'm not usually so—" Brighton waved his hands. "—this."

Gatien sighed. "I remember my signing. My social calendar went from zero to a gazillion in nanoseconds. It was a lot to adjust. And I didn't have some asshole goaltender giving me shit about coming aboard."

Brighton shook his head. "No, you have every right. I understand."

"Do you?"

"Sure. I'm some patsy to get you to crack on the salary negotiations."

"You're also a damn good goaltender. Maybe they want new blood. Maybe it's what they need." He dropped his gaze. "I should be worried."

"No way. You're the best."

"I don't need an ego stroke. It was because of me that we lost in the playoffs."

"Are you kidding me? No one could've stopped that goal. You had three men on you during a power play from a boarding penalty on Christophe, which never should've been called, one of your forwards getting pounded into the boards, and the other one practically beheaded with a clothesline penalty that should have been a game misconduct but was never called. You couldn't have cut down the angle any more than you did. You were all over the net."

"Apparently not. He got it in."

"He kicked it in after play should've been stopped. And the replay showed it didn't completely cross the line. It was a bad call. Three bad calls, actually. Y'all were robbed."

"Newsflash, owners never see it that way. It's just wins and losses. That's it. The calls don't factor in, and the *why* never matters. Owners want trophies and glory and headlines. A team that comes in second place are losers, and losers don't generate cash. And it's *we*, not y'all. You're a part of it."

"You were selected to be part of this year's All-Star team. I wouldn't classify that as being a loser."

Gatien snorted. "That game was a joke. No one takes that shit seriously. That's why they moved it to be played before the championship game." He waved his hands as he spoke. "I mean have you ever seen play stopped because of laughter?"

"Yeah, I've wondered what that was all about. One minute everyone's bunched behind the net, jabbing at the pickle, and the next the ref's blowing the whistle. What happened?"

"It was like the United Nations back there. No one knew what anyone was saying. Players speaking Dutch, German, French, Russian, English, Swedish, Finnish, foolish, and any other kind of *-ish* you can name. Each shouting commands and obscenities while trying to play nicey nice—like that ever happens in hockey. Then Bram Van de Berg's stick went through Veeti Järvinen's blade. While trying to free it, the stick got stuck in Veeti's other skate. Looked more like a cattle roping at a rodeo than a hockey match. Talk about a clusterfuck. It got stupid real quick. I don't know why fans bother to show up, because it's sure not to see hockey."

"Still, it's impressive to be selected."

"Yeah, so much so that Nicco faked an injury not to go. Said his toe was broken. Damn liar." Gatien grinned, illuminating his entire face. "He went skiing the next day."

The twinging between Brighton's thighs repeated, and he shifted uncomfortably. He could get used to gazing at that smile, the row of pearly whites that rested lightly on a plump bottom lip.

Stop daydreaming.

"The coaches didn't say anything to him about it?"

"What were they going to say? It's Nicco. That didn't even register among all the stunts he's pulled." Gatien leaned forward. "The guy actually held auditions for a lookalike and had the double stand in for him on the first day of minicamp. It probably would've worked, too, only he forgot to ask if his double could skate."

Brighton laughed. "Now that's funny as all get-out. Creative, too."

"Yeah, that's probably why he didn't get fined more than he did."

"There seem to be some real characters on the team."

"There are, which makes me wonder what quirks you're going to bring."

"Me? Nah." Brighton shook his head. "I got nothing. I'm pretty boring."

"Really?" Gatien reclined in his chair. "I think you're being modest. Everyone brings something."

"Not me."

"Not true. You already brought something tonight— your friend."

"Dylan? He's never been to a party with celebrities and wanted to tag along. And since he's my roommate, I didn't figure anyone would notice. Obviously, I didn't know I was going to be put on stage and have him join me."

"Roommate?" The way Gatien enunciated the word caused Brighton to shift again. "He's gay, right?"

"Kinda hard to miss, don't you think?"

"So, does that mean you're...?" Gatien didn't complete his sentence.

And there it was. Not that Brighton hid in the closet, but it wasn't a topic he'd discussed. And until he'd befriended Dylan, it wasn't a question he'd been asked. He was comfortable being a gay man, but it didn't need to be the world's business. His agent had warned him that once he went pro, the media would dig and likely exploit the issue, but that was the least of Brighton's concerns, which he had more of than a legless centipede.

"Yeah," Brighton replied, then waited for a reaction.

"Then Dylan's your partner?"

"No, he's my roommate. I don't have a partner."

"I see." Gatien paused for several moments, then asked, "Why not?"

"Why not what?"

"Why don't you have a partner?"

Brighton's eyes widened. That wasn't a question he'd expected. Was it even polite to ask? Surely, Emily Post's etiquette listed it as a faux pas. His own mother didn't ask him that. Of course, she wouldn't. He pulled his collar to soak up the sweat at his nape. "Geez, I don't know. I haven't found anyone?"

"You're asking or telling me?"

Brighton shrugged. "I don't know why." Well, actually, he did if he were honest with himself. "I just don't."

"Well, that's good."

What? "What?"

"Your desserts," the waitress announced.

Damn her bad timing. Brighton swore under his breath as Gatien talked with the waitress, whom he addressed as Holly.

Holly needs to go on somewhere.

However, the longer Brighton thought about it, he hypothesized that Gatien didn't want any negative publicity for the franchise. Some things hadn't changed all that much in the sporting world, and being gay was one of them. All the anti-discrimination laws in the universe wouldn't change the hearts of some people—usually the self-right-eous, moral consciousness of communities. One player's personal issues could easily transform into a distraction for the entire squad.

He stabbed his bread pudding with his spoon, shoveled a manly portion into his mouth, and sighed without real-izing it.

"Good, isn't it?" Gatien asked.

"Mm."

"Gretchen will be happy to hear it. She's a feedback junkie. No matter how good she is, she always craves valida-tion." Without invitation, Gatien reached across the table and scooped a spoonful of the pudding. "I have a dessert Achilles' heel," he confessed. "As a child, I wanted to live in Willy Wonka's chocolate factory."

"I do, too."

"Yeah? Well, there's a new dessert bar on Rue du Compendium. We should go sometime."

"Sure," he replied.

Wait. What? Did Gatien just invite me on a date? Impossible. Couldn't have. I have to get my act together. I'm losing it.

"How about tomorrow?"

"Uh... sounds good." *Sounds like a date.* "Are you...?"

"Am I what?"

"Sure it's a good place?" Brighton inquired, losing his nerve to ask the real question. If he asked and was wrong, oh boy! He'd look like the biggest fool this side of the Pontchartrain. But of course, he was wrong, because there was no way he could be right. Nothing else made sense. For crying aloud, it was Gatien Glesseau.

"Yeah." Gatien nodded, his voice laced with a dash of

something that resembled disappointment. "I've never been, but the reviews are great. If it's anything like the one in New Orleans, it's platinum. I've had it on my to-do list since its grand opening but haven't had an opportunity to make it yet. I got sidetracked by the inconvenience better known as the playoffs. Hell, for all it was worth, I could've blown it off. But there's nothing standing in the way now."

Brighton, you fool, what were you thinking? He's a foodie who likes company. Nothing more. Idiot.

Idiot or not, Brighton had agreed. The flight urge returned, but the predicament between his thighs prevented him from standing. *Utterly ridiculous.* Only the table allowed him to maintain his dignity. He had no choice but to wait until it subsided—unless he used the menu as a shield, hobbled to the restroom, and rubbed one out.

He considered the idea. It wouldn't take long. He had months of pent-up frustration stored, so a couple of quick jerks and he'd be shooting for the ceiling. He even had a condom tucked in his wallet that he could use to conceal the evidence. Of course, for as long as he'd had it, it might've been dry rotted. He could always use a wad of paper towels as backup.

Okay, now you've really plunged off the deep end without scuba gear.

He looked up at Gatien, who observed him with a just entered the *Twilight Zone* stare.

Yes, I am as crazy as you're thinking.

"The heat again?" Gatien asked.

"Yeah." He knew Gatien didn't buy the flimsy excuse, but if he could get away with using it, he would. "But this'll help." He pointed at the bread pudding. Any diversion would, really. Heavens knew he needed the distraction. "I haven't had bread pudding since my grandma died years ago when I was a kid. She used to make it at Christmas. It had a cherry sauce. I think she got the recipe from her mother." Brighton chuckled at the memory. "She used to serve it with a scoop of vanilla bean ice cream on top and in mugs with the most grotesque elf faces on them—which were really gnomes or trolls, but Nanan insisted were elves."

You're rambling. Why wouldn't his mouth stop?

"The spoons were shaped like miniature shovels," he continued. "We'd move from the dinner table to the den and sit in front of our faux log fire while someone read *'Twas the Night Before Christmas* aloud. It's probably the only tradition we ever had. It didn't matter what was going on, we could always depend on Nanan's bread pudding for Christmas dinner."

"Why'd it stop?"

"Huh?"

"The tradition. You used past tense."

"I think maybe we tried, but it wasn't the same after she died. No one had bothered to learn the recipe, and as we each got older, no one took much interest in listening to a kid's poem."

"The entire point of tradition is to hang on to the past—to hold and cherish the child in us and pass it along."

"Sometimes childhood is what people want to forget."

Oops! Not something he wished to discuss.

Gatien's eyebrows shot upward.

"I hear a lot of new start-ups have developed on Rue du Compendium since they have the new streetcar line running," he stated before Gatien could question his reply. "I didn't think they'd ever finish construction. Having to deal with the detoured traffic during rush hour was no joke. Used to take me forever to get home." He ate another bite of his pudding. "This is really good. I'll have to tell Dylan about this place. He doesn't eat sweets often, but he'd enjoy this."

Oh, for the love of Pete, shut the hell up. Where was a case of laryngitis or a punch in the throat when he needed one? He glanced at his empty beer and wished it would magically refill.

Then again, beer isn't strong enough for tonight. Pass the bleach.

5

BRIGHTON ADJUSTED HIS SEAT BELT, gripped the sports car's armrest, and suppressed his urge to hurl. Puking was all he needed to end his night, embarrassing himself yet again and pissing him off for wasting a good meal. But damn, Gatien drove like a short-nosed bat being chased by Satan on rollerblades out of the lower bowels of hell. He busted the speed limit by more than twenty miles an hour, considered stop signs optional, and viewed brakes as an extraneous feature.

The German engine roared down the winding roads edged with ancient oak, blooming magnolias, and hosts of boutiques featuring glittering window displays and flashing neon signs. Although Gatien took curves on all fours—at least Brighton thought all the tires remained touching the pavement, though he couldn't swear to it—the wheels squealed for compassion. Cool air blasted from the vents, granting Brighton a slight reprieve from his internal furnace. However, each time he glanced at Gatien—and heaven forbid the speedometer—his heart thumped, body tremored, and throat tightened. The car wasn't the only thing with a racing engine. He just didn't understand why.

Normally, Brighton enjoyed puzzles and deciphering the wheels that set objects in motion. After all, part of a goalie's job was reading others, which was a type of puzzle and more scientific than most thought. It involved analyzing each part of the body, every subtle movement in anticipation of the next. Generally, he didn't find it complicated— watch the shift of the eyes, position of the hands, and sway of the hip. It was almost formulaic, just plug everything in and achieve an answer. And Brighton experienced an exhilaration each time he figured it out. But usually, the mystery didn't involve him. He knew his role and the part he played. This broke the rules.

True, he was a fan of Gatien's. For years he'd watched him play—how he spread-eagled across the net, not in a splay of desperation or wishfulness but of mastery and skill. Brighton couldn't help but be in awe and initially attributed the charge he'd gotten from Gatien as one of admiration. That made sense. But what didn't make sense was his current feelings that went beyond that.

From the moment in the bar when he'd briefly touched Gatien's chest, sporting ability—at least, not the kind played on the ice—hadn't been on Brighton's mind. He'd be lying if he refused to admit that Gatien's handsomeness had gone unnoticed. Seeing Gatien as more than a sports idol wasn't what threw Brighton. It was the intensity of his attraction, of wanting to know Gatien better, how a small glance made him horny as all giddy up. No man had ever affected him this way. The man across from him ignited a wildfire within him by doing nothing more than breathing, and Brighton remained powerless to control his reaction, like a hormone-injected pubescent. There he was, a professional athlete with a schoolboy crush on his teammate. If that didn't dredge up a heaping helping of manure, Brighton was clueless as to what did.

Gatien clasped the gearshift, moving it from fourth to fifth, rousing further inappropriate imagery and clandestine fantasies from Brighton. Such a powerful, muscular hand with a webbing of bluish veins scarcely visible beneath the surface.

What would it feel like twisted in my hair and—

Brighton clenched his jaw. *Hang on, this is going to be one hell of a bumpy ride home, Toto. This ain't Kansas, and he's no cowardly lion—although he definitely could be a king of the jungle. Oooh oooh eee ah ah ah.*

Gatien glanced at his passenger and laughed, making the enchanting angles of his face even more striking. "What?"

Dear God! His eyes grew wide. "I said that aloud, didn't I?"

"Yeah, you did," Gatien answered, still laughing. "Do I want to know?"

"No, you really don't." *Melting through the floorboard right about now would be excellent.* Of all the humiliating acts he'd executed tonight, making monkey sounds topped the list. "I need some sleep." *And Xanax with an octane boost.* Who was he kidding? He'd never get to sleep tonight. "I'm kinda having an off night?"

"Well, it's not too late for you to get it on."

Now *that* provoked an image.

Oxygen rushed down Brighton's windpipe and he sputtered, alternating between hacking coughs and spasmodic strangles. Sharp thumps pushed outward from his bronchioles against his ribcage. How could a person fuck up breathing? That topped the mortification of imitating a chimpanzee. *Shit!*

"Do you want me to pull over so you can puke?"

"No. Don't. I'd probably get run over by a tractor trailer." *On second thought....* He clasped his chest. "I'm—"

"Fine," Gatien completed. "I know. It's your motto. And tractor trailers don't travel this route. The streets are too narrow and the bridges too low. One false move and eighteen wheels are going tumbling."

"I guess that makes me safe, then."

Gatien shrugged a shoulder. "Well, I don't know about all that. I suppose safe enough for the time being."

Pardon? Brighton's recently unknotted stomach re-knotted. *That was most definitely a pass... I think.*

Having built the courage, he parted his lips to question it when his cell blared the opening chords to AC/DC's "Hells Bells." He didn't need to look to know the caller. Groping in his pants pocket, he fished out the phone and swiped the screen to disconnect.

"You're not going to get that?"

"No."

For several miles, silence reigned until Gatien spoke again. "So, who's Mike?"

Brighton rolled his eyes. He should've guessed Gatien read the incoming call name on the phone screen.

"No one I'm going to talk to right now."

"So, it's like that."

"Yep." Brighton nodded.

"Is he the reason the roommate is just a roommate?"

Brighton turned to stare out the window and considered the complexity of the answer. "I don't wish to discuss it. Besides, why are you so interested?"

"What do you mean why?"

"I mean, it doesn't concern you." From his peripheral vision, he watched Gatien's eyes darken. *Or maybe it does.* "Turn left at the corner. It's the yellow house with the fence."

The car rolled to a stop, and Brighton hopped out before things became any more tense—not that the night had been all lollipops and gumdrops. "I'll meet you tomorrow," he stated, closing the door.

Gatien lowered the passenger window, a strange expression on his face. "No, I'll pick you up. Say, seven?"

Brighton paused. He'd assumed they'd meet around noon for lunch. Seven o'clock was dinnertime, which usually translated to a date.

He took a step backward, his heart jerking into double time. "Sure. Seven."

With a nod, Gatien raised the window and sped off into the darkness, and Brighton turned to face the house, more confused than ever. The porch light was on, which meant Dylan had returned. *Porch light on so I can see, good. Dylan's home, probably wanting to talk, not good.* He always wanted to talk. Generally, Brighton didn't mind, but lately, since Brighton entered the draft, Dylan's "chats" had become more intrusive and Dylan himself clingier. He inserted himself in nearly all aspects of Brighton's life.

Somewhere between the curb and the front door, Brighton decided not to mention his invitation to the dessert bar. And why should he? He didn't want Dylan tagging along on his... *date.*

Brighton grinned and shook his head in disbelief. "This is crazy. There's no way I have a date with Gatien Glesseau."

He positioned his key for the lock, but the door swung

open first. Dylan, bearing a look of disgust and wearing a red kimono robe, blocked his path.

"Where have you been?" he demanded. "I've called you at least a dozen times."

"None of them came through. I must've put my phone on airplane mode on the streetcar and knocked it off on the ride home."

Dylan's eyes narrowed accusingly. "You didn't take the streetcar, unless it's a Transformer and converts to what looked like a very expensive sports car."

"I missed my stop and got a ride home."

"From a stranger?"

"No. Oddly enough, I ran into Gatien, and he gave me a lift."

"Gatien? The man you wanted to avoid? He gave you a ride home?"

"Yes, Dylan, that's how it worked out. Now please let me in. I'm worn slap out and need a shower."

"Why do you need a shower?"

"To maintain good hygiene." He brushed past his roommate.

"You sure that's all?" Dylan approached Brighton and sniffed.

"Cut it out!"

"Touchy."

"How would you like it if I did that to you?"

Dylan grinned. "I wouldn't mind at all, sugarplum." He tightened the belt on his robe. "But you wouldn't do that to anyone. You're a defensive player, right? You stand in the same spot and wait on others' decisions before you do anything."

Brighton wouldn't argue. For one, he didn't feel like it, and two, Dylan had a point. "If you're talking about hockey,

I stand in front of the net," he grumbled, then shuffled toward his room. He kicked his bedroom door closed, stripped, and padded to the bathroom, where he perched on the side of the claw-foot tub while it filled with water. He wasn't a fan of the old-fashioned tub, but he figured a hot bath might be more relaxing than a shower.

He slipped into the tub and sank until the water lapped his chin. Closing his eyes, he curled his toes while the water acted as a balm to soothe his drained muscles and pulsing thoughts of Gatien. He flattened his hands on his lower abdomen where his pubic curls began. He could give into the fantasy and relieve himself of the basic urges plaguing him but decided not to. What use was it to waste time investing in fantasies that had no chance of coming true? That would only lead to more disappointment, and he'd experienced enough of that—although he didn't dare rate his disappointment as being more profound than others. On the contrary, he had to count his blessings. He'd been fortunate, a lucky one. Blessed.

If one looked closely, silver linings were never difficult to find. For example, he'd bumped into Gatien, and they'd been able to come to a truce—at least temporarily. And they had plans for dinner... well, dessert. It would provide an opportunity for him to redeem himself for his behavior for the majority of the night. Now that he'd met with his teammates, the adrenaline surge wouldn't be as severe. Hopefully. Despite a rough start, talking to Gatien had been rather pleasant, and he'd enjoyed spending time with him. He would've enjoyed it more had it been on him. In him.

Stop it.

An odd high-pitched humming sound came from outside, followed by a series of thumps and rattles. Then a split-second boom like a cannon sounded, and the room went black. Climbing from the tub, Brighton fumbled through the dark for a towel and wrapped it around his waist. He made his way to the door, slipping on the tile flooring and leaving a trail of puddles in his wake.

"Dylan," he called from the doorway, "what happened?"

"I don't know. Looks like the entire neighborhood is out."

A loud crash came from the direction of the kitchen that resembled pots and pans. Brighton hoped the stainless-steel percolator coffeepot wasn't included in the racket.

"Are you okay?" he inquired.

"Peachy."

More clattering sounded.

"Okay, then I'm going to bed." He closed the door and found his way to his bed. After quickly drying himself, he crawled under the covers. Soon his mind drifted to his sexy coworker again, his hand moving to the area between his thighs.

"No," he moaned, forcing himself to stop. "I won't." He refused to use Gatien as masturbatory material. Once that started, he'd want more.

Flipping, he pressed his face into the pillow and drifted to sleep in minutes. However, three hours into a dream involving an erotic encounter—hands roving, tongues tangling, groins aching—with a goaltender whose face was obscured by a mask and body obscured by nothing, a stabbing pain near Brighton's elbow jolted him from his slumber into a painful consciousness.

He groaned at having his dream pre-empted by the pain and clicked the switch on the lamp, though the room remained dark. Clearly the power hadn't been restored. The pain worsened in his arm, and Brighton rotated it to alleviate the stiffness. Thinking his sleeping position may have cut off the circulation in his arm, he shifted. With his other arm, he fanned his face, prickling with the heat that had built from the lack of air conditioning.

His actions provided some relief, and he squeezed his eyes shut, focusing on returning to sleep and hoped to resume his dream.

6

BRIGHTON WOKE BONDED to his fitted sheet by sweat. The top sheet lay bunched on the floor where he'd kicked it off during the night. Awaking in such a state wasn't unusual, but the why was. Still no power, and the house's temperature had kicked up to a miserable level. According to the automated message from the power company's outage line, the energy company was aware of the problem and would possibly restore power some time before the next millennium.

But despite the heat, Brighton shivered, and his head felt as if a corset had been laced around his skull. An incredible pressure pushed at the backs of his eyes that hurt even his eyelashes, and he could barely take two steps before feeling winded. Two years before, he'd caught the flu and experienced similar symptoms, but these were magnified by a couple of thousand. Aside from general joint pain, his elbow throbbed in a rhythm of *ouch, ouch, fuck* every few seconds. He had some movement of his arm, but the avocado-size lump made it virtually immobile. From the position, the only way Brighton could view the lump was in the mirror, and what an ugly sight it was. His skin was indented like the texture of a tangerine and glowed a shiny red. Not the best start for a rookie goalie.

Ordinarily, he would've toughed it out on the couch, but with no air conditioning and a possible pending date later, Brighton caught the streetcar to his doctor's office without an appointment. Sure, he could've seen one of the team's doctors, but Dr. Janson had been seeing him since he was a kid. At the time, she was a resident awaiting admission to a general surgery fellowship program, and although she'd specialized since then, Brighton kept her as his primary physician. They had a history, and she would tell him like it was. Lots of doctors lied—well, maybe not lied, but definitely misled—children. They would say things like "This won't hurt a bit," then ram a steel beam into a vein to pump out a gallon of blood. Dr. Jan would say, "This is going to hurt like hell, kid." However, the real reason Brighton liked her so much was that she still gave him suckers after his visits. And not just any suckers—she had the good stuff, Swirl Saf-T-Pops. Yum. She'd pump him full of some go-go juice and ensure he'd be in mint condition by night.

"That's going to require lancing and drainage," Dr. Janson stated after one glance. Her lips creased in a stern grimace as she pulled on a pair of blue latex gloves and pushed up her sleeves. "How long have you had this?"

"Popped up overnight."

"With no other indications?"

"Well, I felt a little stiffness. What is it?"

"A big wad of nasty." She lightly pressed on the lump and Brighton nearly hopped off a table. He'd taken jabs with hockey sticks that hurt less. "I'll have to culture it, but my guess is MRSA, Meth—"

"Methicillin-resistant Staphylococcus aureus. I remember." How could he forget? He looked around the room, thinking it hadn't changed much over the years. "But what is this?" He moved his elbow.

"Doesn't look like any type of bite," the doctor responded, examining the area closer. "Have you scraped your arm on anything?"

"Not that I'm aware."

"And otherwise how have you been feeling? Any fatigue? Malaise?"

"Only after practice."

The doctor smiled. "Congratulations on your draft. I always knew you would make it."

Brighton grinned back at her but wrinkled his nose at the smell of the astringent. "As a hockey player?"

"That too." She tapped his shoulder. "Lie back on the pillow and prop your arm this way so I can deaden the area." She waited until he complied, then draped a chux pad beneath his arm before rattling instructions to her nurse. "You were a tough kid."

"Hospital food does that." He flinched as the needle sank into his skin. The anesthesia burned at the injection site. "Is this really necessary?"

"You'll thank me later. How are you sleeping?"

"On my back mostly. Occasionally on my side."

"You eating regularly?"

"Yep. As many empty calories as I can get my hands on. In fact, I'm going to a dessert bar later today."

"No, sir." Dr. Jansen shook her head. "You're going straight home and to bed."

"Bed?" Brighton frowned. "Why? Because of a bump?"

"Because you're sick." She stuck the needle in him again. "You have a fever of 104 and an infection. This is an abscess, and the surrounding tissue is necrotizing. You're likely septic. I'll order blood work to be sure. And if that's the case, I will admit you."

Fever? Septic? He knew he'd been feeling hotter than usual, and a headache, but he associated that with other matters. "But I have a da—business meeting later."

A discerning gleam flickered in her eyes. "I thought you said you were going to a dessert bar."

"Yes, for a business-like meeting." Well, it was nearly true. If he played his cards right, he might handle some business.

"You'll have to change your plans. After the procedure, you'll need to drink plenty of fluids and rest."

"You gotta be kidding me."

"Afraid not. You've got a critical infection. I'm surprised you're functioning as well as you are. Most people wouldn't be walking around, let alone being stubborn with their physician."

"Can't be that significant in comparison," he muttered.

"Actually, that makes it more so and doubles my concern. With a weakened immune system, things can go south quickly."

"You don't get much more southern than South Louisiana. I'll be fine. Stick a Band-Aid on it and I'll be on my way."

She disposed of the syringe in the biohazard waste receptacle. "Brighton, either you give me your word that you'll stay home and rest, or I'll admit you to the hospital for three days."

"Three days?"

"That's right." She held up three fingers. "Three."

"That's blackmail."

"That's the way it's going to be. Besides, if it's only business, you can have a teleconference. I'll write you a note."

"But it's a bump. It's not much bigger than a mosquito"—*the size of a pterodactyl*—"bite. There's got to be an alternative."

"There isn't unless you want to wait around until I have to amputate your arm."

"Fine. You're so dramatic."

She applied pressure to his upper arm. "Can you feel that?"

"Barely."

"Good. Turn your head and face the wall. This isn't for the faint of heart."

Oh please. He was a hockey player. He'd seen blood splatter for yards.

Initially, he obeyed and looked away. However, curiosity—the same serial killer that slaughtered all those cats—soon took over. He turned to watch Dr. Jansen and lost his breakfast at the sight.

BRIGHTON'S INTENTION had been to call Dylan. But when he retrieved his phone to do so, his thumb swiped against the screen, unintentionally answering the incoming call from Gatien to confirm their dessert plans. Brighton hadn't planned on mentioning being in a doctor's office, but the clinic's PA system in the background ousted his location. *Why are those things so obnoxiously loud anyway?*

Inventing an elaborate tale to hide his whereabouts required too much effort. Therefore, Brighton stuck with the truth and admitted being sprawled on an examination table. He did, however, omit the hurling incident.

Twenty minutes later, while still waiting to ensure there were no negative side effects of the antibiotic and sucking on his lollipop, Brighton's eyes bulged when Gatien entered the examination room.

"What are you doing here?" Brighton asked.

"You said on the phone that your doctor wouldn't discharge you until you found someone to drive you home. You have a ride yet?"

"Not really. I left a message for my roommate, but he hasn't returned my call."

"Well then," Gatien replied smugly, "there's your answer."

"I could call a taxi."

"Or you could say thank you."

Brighton lowered his gaze an inch and swallowed thickly. "Thank you."

Gatien motioned to Brighton's arm bandaged with neon green gauze. "What's going on there?"

Brighton shrugged. "I don't know. But whatever it is, I got a boll of cotton"—what Dr. Jansen termed an antiseptic wick—"crammed in it, and it doesn't tickle. I suppose I'll live for now, though."

"Can you leave?"

"I have to wait for the nurse. My doctor is holding my prescriptions hostage until she sees for herself that someone came for me." He swung his dangling legs. "But honestly, I'm not in any hurry to get home. The power went out last night, and it was hot as a July barbecue in Hades when I left this morning. I assume it's still off. The power company is supposed to call when it's been restored, but they haven't."

"You can hang out at my place."

Brighton's heart skipped several beats. "I couldn't do that."

"Why not? I don't have cooties," Gatien replied, eyeballing the sucker darting in and out of Brighton's mouth.

Laughter barreled from Brighton before he could stop it. "I don't want to impose."

"If it was an imposition, I wouldn't have offered. Now, what do we need to do to spring you from this joint?"

We? I could get used to that.

"Is this going to be okay with Gretchen?"

"What does my sister have to do with anything? Last time I checked, she wasn't living there—especially not with her two 'I can scream at the top of my lungs longer than you can stand it' hellions—and she damn sure isn't paying the mortgage."

Sister? Now that's a game changer.

Maybe Brighton's radar hadn't been as off as he thought. Perhaps Gatien had asked him on a date after all, and at present, he could swear Gatien tracked the lollipop that left a sugary sheen on his lips as it darted in and out of his mouth.

No, that still couldn't be right. Gatien was constantly photographed with beautiful women draped on his arms. And last summer there had been a scandal about him having a notorious affair with Darla Richards, fiancée to Harper Kincaid, the racecar driver/reality television star from *MotorCaid*. In fact, the rumor alleged the producers considered canceling the show unless the affair ended. Apparently, Darla and Harper had sorted their differences because the show was renewed for another season, and the couple relocated from Saint Anne to Atlanta.

Brighton stilled his legs and studied Gatien. He would

hydroplane into insanity if he didn't quit fantasizing. Yet something nagged him that a possibility existed.

Dr. Jansen entered, her expression grimmer than before. "How's the patient?"

"Ready to be paroled." Brighton motioned to Gatien. "My bail has been posted."

Dr. Jansen introduced herself to Gatien, extended her hand to shake, and then gave him a thorough once-over. Brighton suspected Gatien had that effect on most women. And who could blame them? He was the type of man who women ogled as their mouths watered, taking in all six feet five inches of sculpted muscle and the mass of wavy ebony locks that brushed his collar.

"One of your lab reports came back. I want to discuss it with you."

"I'll step out," Gatien stated, but failed to move toward the door.

Dr. Jansen shook her head. "If you'll be the person helping Brighton, you'll need to know how to provide care and treat the wound."

"Yes, I'll be the person," Gatien replied.

Whoa! Brighton's thoughts somersaulted and splintered in too many directions for him to keep track of them all. Not only was he being portrayed as some invalid, but Gatien was being designated as his caregiver? This was about as jacked up as bootlegged cable TV with a jailbroken remote.

Brighton stiffened. "I can take care of it myself."

Dr. Jansen held up three fingers, and Brighton ceased his protest. "As discussed earlier, you are indeed septic, and the infection is deep in the tissue. I'll prescribe a strong antibiotic, but if you get worse or are showing no improvement in twenty-four hours, you'll need to come back for IV treatment."

Brighton lips twisted in disgust. "I'm not staying in the hospital."

Ignoring Brighton, Dr. Jansen faced Gatien. "If he continues to have a fever, chills, becomes disoriented, or the incision is hot to the touch with additional swelling, bring him to the ER. Otherwise, the dressing will need to be changed three times a day. You'll need to remove the antiseptic wick and repack the wound." She grabbed a tablet from the counter and showed Gatien a short video demonstrating the procedure. "My nurse will ensure you have all the supplies you need before you leave. He's to remain in bed with no extraneous activities or physical exertion."

"Isn't that a little kind of overkill?" Brighton complained.

"And don't worry. I'm also prescribing something for pain once the anesthesia wears off. It'll put him to sleep and give you a nice long break from his grumbling." She shot a wicked grin at Brighton.

"That's not funny."

"Oh, it's not meant to be. I know what an obstinate patient you can be. Any questions?"

"No," Gatien replied. "I got it."

She typed something into the tablet and then reached into her pocket. "If you don't have any problems, I want to see you in my office next week for a follow-up." She handed Brighton another lollipop. "Here's one for the road." Then she gave one to Gatien. "And here's one for you for having to put up with him."

After Dr. Jansen left the room, Gatien turned to face Brighton and grinned. "I like her."

Ah, an opening. "She's single."

"That's nice."

Seriously? That's all he's going to give me? Brighton

parted his lips to suggest Gatien ask her out, but then the nurse entered with a large brown bag, several papers, and a wheelchair.

"What in tarnation is all that?" Brighton asked.

"These are the supplies you'll need. It's enough to get you started. I have a list of everything you'll need to purchase from the pharmacy. Your prescriptions have been called in. And this"—she pointed to the wheelchair—"is your luxurious transport to the parking lot."

"This is nuts. I'm not using that."

Brighton slid from the table and was immediately dizzy. Voices muffled, and the room went out of focus. He wavered until he felt a strong grip tighten at his waist and give him balance.

"Oh, you're using it," Gatien insisted.

Brighton's eyes snapped at the authoritative tone in Gatien's voice that summoned a tingle of fear blended with excitement. He froze momentarily, taken aback by the command. But Brighton had never been known to back down. He attempted another step with similar results, stumbling over a chair.

Okay, perhaps I need to reconsider the wheelchair. And to think, one bump caused all this ruckus.

7

WATER.

Brighton pried his tongue from the roof of his mouth and smacked his chapped lips as he snuggled into the pillowtop mattress. The cotton sheets pressed cool and soft against his skin. He wasn't ready to be awake, but the scratch in his throat insisted he do just that. However, he decided he could wait five more minutes... until the smell of buttery popcorn and cologne invaded his nostrils, and crunching cracked the silence.

Huh?

Brighton's eyes popped open. He remembered waiting at the pharmacy and being led into Gatien's living room. He even remembered something about the guest bedroom being used as an office. What he didn't remember was getting naked, which he was. What was more, he felt movement to his left.

He wasn't alone.

Holy hell, what happened?

He shook his head in an attempt to clear the cloud over his memory. Clutching the top sheet, he held it steadfast at his waist until he flipped onto his back and stared upward at the rotating ceiling fan. The speed was slow enough that he could distinguish the individual blades.

"How are you feeling?"

Gatien. Oh God, I'm in bed with Gatien—nekkid as a jaybird!

"Uh... I don't know. I seem to be in a... state."

Gatien's gaze turned from the muted television and washed over Brighton from head to toe, pausing at the noticeable tent in the sheet at his groin. "Seems that way."

Brighton's cheeks grew warm. He'd meant his lack of clothes, not his throbbing dick. But since Gatien brought it up... literally...

Ah shit! Not this again.

"Any idea how I got like this?"

"I suppose the way biology dictated it." He licked butter from his fingers. "Want to do something about it?"

"What?" Brighton choked on his tongue.

"I asked," Gatien repeated, enunciating slowly, "if you wanted to do something about it."

"Something like what?"

Gatien smirked. "You need me to spell it out for you?"

"In a word, yes. No. Shit."

Gatien's lips parted, confident and calculated.

"You know what? Forget it." Brighton slid up in the bed, leaned against the headboard, and pressed his index fingers against his temples. "What happened to my clothes?"

"You took them off."

"*I* took them off?"

"Yes." Gatien set the bowl of popcorn on a nightstand beside the bed. "I asked if you wanted to lie down, and you said you'd be comfortable on the canapé. About an hour later, you said you were hot, removed your clothes, crawled into the bed, and fell asleep."

"No, I wouldn't have." But he had. The memory emerged, and a flush swam up his neck. Pain medication often made him loopy, but he could honestly swear he'd never done anything this cockamamie. "Why didn't you stop me? Kick me out or something?"

"You're not hurting anything. Besides, I figured you needed the rest. You've been out for nearly twelve hours."

"No way!" Brighton looked at the radio clock on the armoire, the digital red numbers seemingly mocking him.

"Are you hungry? I ordered Chinese. They didn't have chicken noodle soup, but I got the egg drop, assuming it would be close enough. It's the same animal, I think. Although, they may use duck eggs. It's still fowl. The restaurant doesn't close until midnight, so I can order the sweet and sour if you want."

Brighton shook his head. "I need some water."

"Coming up." Gatien swung his long legs over the edge of the bed.

"No, I'll get it," Brighton insisted. "I need to move around."

"Are you sure? Because last time you tried, you nose-dived into the floor. I have white carpeting in the living room. That'll be a bitch to clean up, and the maid doesn't come until Tuesday, although she's a really horrible maid. She's an older lady and usually forgets things." He shrugged. "But she reminds me of my grammy, so what can I do? I can't fire my grammy."

This situation wasn't typical by any stretch of the imagination, so how was it that Gatien behaved as if there was nothing unusual about having a naked stranger in his bed? Granted, Brighton wasn't some vagrant plucked from the streets or a floozy whose number he'd gotten from a gas station restroom stall, but neither did he know Gatien on this level.

Well, apparently, he did now, considering he was the nude one of the two. Then again, Gatien probably had frequent hookups. He was a good-looking man with high visibility and a stash of cash. It wouldn't be difficult for him to find willing participants. The thought irritated Brighton more than it should have.

"Yes, I'm better now. Your carpet is safe," Brighton replied.

Tugging the sheet around his waist, Brighton padded to the chair where his clothes were neatly folded, dressing in his boxers and sweatpants. He'd worry with the rest later, but for now, he needed to get some circulation going and brain activity functioning. Being that close to Gatien sent Brighton's innards haywire.

He wandered out of the bedroom and from room to room in the spacious house, pausing periodically to look at the neoclassical artwork adorning the walls, until he located the kitchen—lots of counter space, but the only visible small appliances were a single-cup coffeemaker and a compact microwave. Obviously, it wasn't a room that saw much use.

He opened the refrigerator and viewed his drinking choices. The selection was slim, between a six-pack of draft, a mostly empty two-liter soda, and a sports drink. Ordinarily, he wouldn't take the last of anything in his host's home, but this was no ordinary situation. He opened the bottle and consumed the sports drink in two long gulps. Instead of closing the refrigerator door, he shut his eyes and allowed the cool air to drift over his bare torso.

"I thought you said you felt better."

Brighton startled and tensed but didn't open his eyes. "I do."

"Then why are you standing here in the dark with the fridge door open?"

"Cooling off."

"We should take your temperature again."

We. Brighton grinned to himself. "I don't have a fever."

He heard Gatien move forward, felt the heat of his body closing the space between them.

"So why do you need cooling off?"

Why the hell do you think?

"'Cause I'm hot and bothered." Shit! He didn't mean to say that aloud. But since he had... "All these mixed signals. I mean, you must know that some of the things you've said to a man of my persuasion can be interpreted in an unintended way."

"Then allow me to clarify for you."

Gatien placed his palm above Brighton's hip, slid it around to his navel, and allowed his fingers to deftly stroke the trail of honey-brown hair that vanished beneath the band of the sweatpants.

Hello! The bottled drink tumbled from Brighton's hand and landed with a plastic *crackle*.

He relaxed into Gatien's broad chest. Moving forward again, Gatien pressed his firm erection against Brighton's rear and leaned over to place light kisses from his shoulder blade to the sensitive spot below his earlobe. He continued moving his palm downward, dipping his fingers beneath the elastic into the thatch of hair and skimming the bulging knob straining against the cotton fabric before easing it out with both hands.

"Is it getting clearer?" Gatien whispered, gliding the

heel of his palm down Brighton's shaft while his lower region gyrated against Brighton's backside.

"Most definitely." Brighton raised his arms over his shoulders and wrapped them around Gatien's neck while angling his head to meet Gatien's lips. They tasted of a sweet, exotic candy tangled with butter. At first, Gatien's smooth lips brushed against Brighton's as if uncertain, then firmly pressed before opening and slipping his tongue inside. Heat skittered down Brighton's arms and his entire body ached with want. The kiss quickly transformed from tentative to impatient. "Don't stop."

"You're really thick," Gatien uttered, adding more pressure with his palm. A glimmer of precum beaded on the engorged mushroom head, and Gatien rubbed his thumb around in a dawdling, languorous rhythm to spread it. "I love the feel of you. I could stroke you all night." He gave a jerk with one hand using an overhand grip and fondled Brighton's balls with the other, eliciting an innate growl from Brighton, whose breath had become little more than starts and pants.

"Mercy be," Brighton moaned, his voice mangled in a gargle. He attempted to shift, but Gatien held him still, kneading his taut balls like dough and stroking faster. Brighton's hips betrayingly lurched forward and matched Gatien's speed. Apparently, his libido forgot it was no longer sixteen. "You've got to slow down."

"Uh-uh."

Squirming, Brighton attempted another escape but was at the mercy of Gatien's roving and relentless fingers. The heaviness in Brighton's balls tightened and lifted. Just the warmth of Gatien's sultry mouth was enough to bring Brighton to the edge, yet there was so much more. It caused the blood to hum beneath his skin and his pulse to beat savagely.

"Please, Gatien," he moaned, writhing against his hold. His tone bordered on begging, but he was too far gone to care what he sounded like. In any minute, he'd be reduced to even less.

"You sound so fucking hot," Gatien murmured.

"Oh gawd! You're going to make me come."

"Good." His eyes intensified with lust and dark amusement.

No, not good. Brighton wanted this to last. He was more than a minute man, but Gatien was forcing him to fight to withstand each millisecond. Sweat glistened on his brow as Brighton struggled, but he knew a losing battle when he encountered one. This was his Custard's last stand, remember the Alamo, and all that fruitless shit.

How was Gatien so controlled when every fiber in Brighton threatened to explode, implode, or some-thingplode?

"Fuck!" A wave of ecstasy formed in Brighton's stomach and crashed over him. He convulsed as long cords of white cream jetted hot and hard onto his stomach and Gatien's hands. His knees buckled as his body went limp, robbed of strength. "Gatien—"

"Shh. I got you," Gatien whispered, playing in the stickiness and massaging it into the younger man's skin. "Enjoy this." He moved one hand to caress his back, causing zaps of excitement to skip through Brighton's body, before twisting in his hair—now a damp mop that hung haphazardly in his face. He tugged lightly, and Brighton didn't resist.

Instead, he looked up at Gatien, his eyes clouded with a post-orgasmic bliss, chest heaving with labored breaths, and lips plump from bruising kisses. He'd never felt small—

although he was one of the smaller players—but the six-inch differential between him and Gatien made him feel like a *pischouette*. A speck. Vulnerable. And those eyes… those gorgeous hazel eyes weakened him further.

Brighton had never been reckless in his relationships—not that a hand job in the middle of a dark kitchen constituted as relationship status. What transpired between them was on the verge of dangerous on multiple levels. This was his teammate, for crying aloud—a teammate whose position he threatened to take.

Well, not really.

Yes, Brighton was good, and his confidence in his playing ability remained strong. But Gatien was seasoned as well as having mega talent. No sane owner would play Brighton over Gatien. However, the current situation had little to do with sanity and centered on money. Money, of course, sometimes made for fools' decisions. And so did lust.

Damn, he wanted this man.

"Why are you doing this?" Brighton asked, his voice barely audible and revealing a glimpse of the emotional mess brewing inside of him. He cast his eyes downward to avoid the obvious desire being discovered and recognized.

"Because."

"Look, I know what you must think of me, but I'm not some damn toy to pacify your pastime or curiosity."

"No, you're no toy." His lips curved as he brushed them over Brighton's hair.

"And I'm not some rebound distraction, either."

Gatien loosened his hold slightly. "Who's rebounding?"

"Don't pretend. Your sexcapades with Darla Richards was all over the media."

"Yeah? Well, the media is stupid. And you shouldn't believe everything you read." He released Brighton. "If you want to know about Darla and me, you should ask. Wasn't it yesterday that you were harping on this very issue?"

Yes. Brighton's features twisted in harsh lines. Damn his own words. "You saying you never had a thing with Darla?"

"No, I didn't. And if I had, what does that have to do with anything now?"

"Because that gleam in your eyes says you're about to fuck me, and I don't want my first time to be a meaningless notch on your bedpost."

"First?" Gatien took a step in retreat.

Damn, where's my filter? Just because it was the truth didn't mean he had to blurt it out like a Catholic confession.

Brighton chuckled, slightly embarrassed. "Don't tell me a virgin scares you."

"No, but... never?"

"Well, you don't have to act so disgusted by it."

"I'm not, it's just that... well... wow." He paused. "Maybe we should slow down."

Brighton tossed his hair over his shoulder and blew out a rushed breath. "Whatever."

Gatien intertwined his fingers with Brighton's and brought their joined hands to his lips. Brighton stared at the spot Gatien's lips touched and marveled at the oddly intimate gesture.

"Don't be that way. We have time."

Gatien gathered Brighton back into his arms and kissed him with a delicious sensation that filled the younger man with warmth and desire. Within seconds, Brighton's lips yielded, and he submitted to Gatien's embrace. Their tongues met, and the tiny hairs along his flesh sent rippling vibrations between his legs.

Screw waiting. I need it now. So be it if this is a meaningless fling for Gatien as long as I can savor it at present.

"I don't need commitment," Brighton assured, tugging at the hem of Gatien's shirt. "I just ask for respect. If I'm nothing, then say it."

"You'll never be nothing."

Brighton's internal switch flipped to overdrive, and his hands roamed everywhere at once—yanking Gatien's T-shirt over his head, rushing jittery fingers across his tattooed arms and chest, and fumbling loose the button fly of his jeans. Goalies had to be quick, and the tricks of the trade came in useful off the ice as well. His hands snaked their way back up Gatien's chest and scraped across his nipples, his tongue following.

Gatien caught Brighton's wrists and held them steady. "Not here."

Before Brighton could answer, Gatien spun and had them both trotting down the hallway to the bedroom, Brighton landing on the mattress without realizing he'd been pushed. In one swift move, his sweats and boxers were heaved off and flying across the room. He maneuvered, avoiding placing pressure on his elbow, and pushed at Gatien's jeans. Somewhere in the tug-of-war, he ended up on top with Gatien's hands pushing his shoulders down-ward. Understanding, he slid down Gatien's body, crouched to his knees between Gatien's thighs, and ran his hands the length of the other man's torso. With a gleam in his eyes, he wet his lips and traced the dorsal vein of Gatien's cock with his fingers before taking the head into his mouth and sucking lightly. Gatien's rumbled moans encouraged Brighton to continue, and he fisted Gatien's shaft in one hand while cradling his balls with the other. He created a taut suction with his mouth and retracted to the tip, where he swirled his tongue in dizzying figure eights. Gatien's hips arched off the mattress, hands fisted in Brighton's hair, and pushed himself fervently into Brighton's mouth. Brighton responded by relaxing his throat and swallowing as much of Gatien as he could.

A carnal growl tumbled from Gatien. "Damn, you give great head."

"You taste good." He delighted in the tender velvetiness of Gatien's cock, and even more in the whimpers his teammate emitted. Yes, he was the reason for the senior goaltender's moans of bliss, and he intended to leave a lasting impression. He gave a couple firmer pulls before vigorously feasting on Gatien's cockhead, ensuring to lick beneath the ridge.

The grunts became a symphony to Brighton's ears, causing his own dick to clench and catapult straight up, pressing and pulsing against his abdomen. While sucking, Brighton used one hand to fist himself.

Dragging the flat of his tongue across the slit did them both in. He felt Gatien's body tense and refused to pull off, allowing Gatien to shoot into his mouth.

"Yes, milk me dry."

Despite his attempts to not lose a drop, it was too much, and Gatien's seed seeped from the corners of Brighton's mouth. The tangy fluid fueled Brighton's own blurring release, and after Gatien's last spurt, Brighton allowed him to slip free. Rocking back on his heels, he raised his eyes to meet Gatien's sated gaze.

"I do believe that was a goal," Brighton said, his voice hoarse. His heart thumped quick and hard in his chest.

Gatien hooked his arms beneath Brighton's and hoisted him onto the bed. "This game is going into OT."

8

DURING INTERMISSION IN REGULATION PLAY, rebuilding energy was not only encouraged but a necessity. Trainers provided carts of carbs and avoided protein. Foods like granola and bananas were the staples, and Brighton disliked bananas wholeheartedly. But none of that was on the menu now during this intermission, and he was sure he'd need a lot more energy than what was required for twenty minutes of skating. Gatien promised to wear him out in half that time.

"They make this look easy on TV," Brighton stated as he fumbled with his chopsticks, the subtle aroma of just-had-sex rolling off his skin.

"Here." Gatien retrieved a dumpling, dipped it into the sauce, and fed it to Brighton.

"Mm. Good." He set the container on the tray, repositioned a pillow behind his lower back, and pointed to a vegetable dish. "What's this?"

"Szechuan green beans. I can't believe you've never had Chinese."

"I've had Chinese, just not this fancy or using these

things." He tossed the chopsticks on the tray, removed another dumpling with his fingers, and popped it in his mouth. "There's a Chinese restaurant across from the campus, but it doesn't serve anything like this."

"I know that place, and it doesn't count. It's not authentic. It's burgers and fries chopped in tiny bites and called dim sum."

"Is there any restaurant in this town you don't know?"

"I'm a foodie." He patted his muscled stomach. "I like eating."

Brighton traced along the bold black ink of a tribal tattoo extending from Gatien's navel to his side. "What's this?"

Gatien smiled. "You like that?"

"Yeah, I do. What's it mean?"

"Truth. Balance. Justice. My motto. It's all I ever ask of anyone."

Brighton snorted. "There's a balance between truth and justice?"

"Mostly. There certainly should be. I'm not much for politics."

"That's very optimistic of you."

"You sound surprised."

"A little. I took you more of a 'half-empty' type guy."

Gatien brushed Brighton's long hair over his shoulder. "What does it matter? As long as there's water in the glass, no one is going to succumb to dehydration. Besides, you don't know me well enough to make those types of assumptions."

"We all make assumptions, Gatien. It's only a matter of how many we make and to what degree. It's called projections and statistics."

"Is that what it's being called these days?"

"What else would you call it?"

"Gossip."

Brighton lowered his eyes a fraction. "I've been following your career and off-season escapades. I guess that makes me kind of a groupie."

"Well, I did meet you at Portmanteau's." Gatien rolled his shoulders and smirked. "That's where most of the lot lizards and puck bunnies hang out."

"Did you really climb K2 twice?"

"I had no other choice. The name demanded it."

"Does that mean you plan on climbing Annapurna II twice as well?"

"Nah, I think I'm pretty much over it. K2 wasn't nearly as exciting the second time. There are other things to do."

A devious smirk sprang to Brighton's lips. "Like bungee jumping above a volcano?"

Gatien matched it with one of his own. "Maybe. But if I had a reason to not go off, I wouldn't."

That sounded promising. "Such as?"

"You figure it out."

A dull buzz resonated from the floor. It took several moments before Brighton realized the sound stemmed from his cell phone in the pocket of his sweatpants. At least it had been there before Gatien slung the pants across the room. *Good thing I have phone insurance.*

He moved to the edge of the mattress but halted beneath Gatien's grasp. "Where are you going?" he griped.

"To answer my phone."

"Now? It's after eleven."

"Sorry, Ma, I didn't know I was on restriction." Brighton climbed out of bed, followed the sound to the armoire, and knelt to retrieve the phone from beneath it. He padded back to the bed, swiped the screen, and swore. Fifty-one missed calls and seventy texts—most from Dylan but also from family, all inquiring about his whereabouts. He opened his contacts and clicked on Dylan's avatar.

"What are you doing now?"

"I have to call someone before they summon the national guard."

"You're a grown man. You've never spent a night away from home?"

"I left Dylan a voice mail that I was at the hospital. I forgot to tell him I was leaving with you." He slid between the Egyptian cotton sheets. "He's probably checking the morgues."

"He has a taste for necrophilia?"

Brighton cast a dirty glare at him.

Gatien snickered. "Wouldn't your doctor have told him?"

"I would think, but—" Brighton cut off his statement when Dylan answered. "Hey."

"Finally! Where the hell are you? I've been blowing up your phone."

"Yeah, I just saw. I've been asleep." *Among other things.*

"On the streetcar?"

"Of course not."

"Mike's been by twice looking for you. Where are you?"

Uh-oh. Brighton glanced at Gatien and bit his lower lip. This was quicksand he preferred not to trudge. Dylan would surely have a commentary—and none too nice, either, especially if he explained that he was Gatien's special experimentation project. An unfinished experiment, he should add. Once they both refueled, Brighton fully intended on... well, what he intended didn't matter.

It seemed Gatien was kind of a Dom, if there was such a thing as "kind of." Granted, no handcuffs had been produced yet, but Brighton bet if he snooped in the night-stands, he'd discover interesting finds. Until then, if this—whatever it was—worked out, they would need to have a discussion about his alpha assertion. But for now, he was okay with Gatien being the one in control. Hell, he was getting fucked and getting fed. Why would he complain? "At Semy's," he lied, blurting the first name that came to mind. Semy was a good alibi. Dylan wouldn't read much into it, and he didn't know Semien well enough to call to verify the story. He couldn't even if he wanted to—he didn't have the number, and Semy wasn't listed. And even if he did manage to find a contact number, Semy wouldn't fink. *Win-win.*

Still, self-reproach and anxiety knotted in Brighton's stomach. He detested lying, especially to close friends.

"Do you need me to swing by and pick you up?"

Gatien overheard the question and frowned. "Don't even think you're leaving here without me getting in that ass."

"What?" Dylan questioned.

Brighton's flesh heated in astonishment and anticipation. "Nothing. That was the TV."

"Oh. Well, the power's still off. I thought maybe you and I could hang out at the all-night mime festival in Le Centre. They have door prizes."

Brighton furrowed his brow. *Fat chance.* "I think I'm going to hang here. Dr. Jan said I should rest." *Yeah, like resting is going to happen.*

"Okay." Dylan's voice deflated. "So, do you want me to come over and hang with you guys? I bought some fresh banana muffins from the bakery down the street."

Banana. Yuck. "There's no need to put yourself out on my account."

"I wouldn't be. It'll be fun sitting around, sipping chardonnay, and talking about sports injuries and what really goes on in the dugout."

"First off, I don't know where you'd be sitting since there aren't any dugouts in hockey. Second, what sports injuries have you ever had? And don't say the time you fell off the treadmill."

"That was a genuine injury." Dylan's indignation radiated through the phone. "I had to go to the ER on a backboard."

"Only because of school policy. You weren't hurt, other than maybe your ego." And the ego part was a stretch. Brighton had watched Dylan revel in the attention and then proceed to shamelessly flirt with one of the paramedics. Brighton had to admit the medic had been cute, but that wasn't the point. Injured patients didn't behave that way— unless they had severe head wounds.

Gatien tapped the back of his bare wrist with his index finger to indicate time. Brighton threw up his index finger in response.

"I could've been," Dylan refuted.

"Anyway, alcohol is off my menu tonight. I'm positive mixing booze and narcotics is on the FDA's naughty list." The phone vibrated in Brighton's hand.

"You don't have to drink."

"Listen, Dylan, my mom's calling on the other line. I'll talk to you later." He disconnected before his roommate could protest. Brighton didn't feel like a lengthy discussion with his mother, either, but he knew she'd be upset and worried. To pacify her, he sent a quick text, informing her that his medical status was nothing dire and he would call in the morning. Then, he tossed the phone on the nightstand nearest him and sighed.

"So, you had an all-points bulletin out for your location?" Gatien inquired. "That happen a lot?"

"Not really. I'm sure Dylan called my mom and got her all worked up for nothing. She's an excessive worrier."

"That's not very convenient for a hockey mom."

"I know, and I've warned Dylan about calling her. But sometimes he doesn't think."

"Or doesn't care."

"I wouldn't say that."

"I would, and I did."

"How do you come to that conclusion?"

"I overheard what he was saying, and never once in the conversation did he ask what was wrong or how we're feeling. Lovers typically do."

"I told you we're not lovers."

"No? Then why didn't you tell him where you were? And who's Mike?"

Brighton looked away toward the bunched sheets between them. "It's complicated."

"Lovers generally are."

Brighton's eyes snapped upward, a fire dancing in them. "It isn't like that."

"There's no reason to explain it to me."

"I like my privacy, okay? And what's it to you, anyway? You really want people to know we're burning holes in your bed? How the wheeling beauty entertains himself in his spare time, getting an adrenaline rush by engaging in the taboo behavior most convenient at the time?"

Gatien packed up two empty cartons, pitched them the short distance into a trash can, and then pointed to Brighton's discarded chopsticks. "You done with those?"

"Sure."

Gathering the remainder of the food containers, he

removed them from the bed, rolled to his side with his back to Brighton, and cocooned himself in the sheet. "I'm going to sleep."

Brighton's libido wailed. "I thought—"

"You thought wrong."

"You seriously can't be upset because—"

"Shut the light off."

Brighton scrubbed his hand down his face and set his jaw, staring at the tattoo cascading from Gatien's shoulder to lower bicep—a colorful, flaming hockey helmet on a fissuring skull with wolfish teeth. *Appropriate for someone so gruff who can turn off and on within seconds.* Power surges took longer than Gatien's mood switching.

Brighton stared at his bedmate for a moment longer before clicking off the light and sliding down in the bed.

"Gatien," he said after several moments of stewing and his body beginning to relent, "you really are an ass."

"I know," he replied. Sleep already had crept into his voice.

Brighton snatched the cell from the nightstand and opened a new message to Semien.

If anyone should ask, I'm crashing at your place tonight.

That makes for an awkward threesome came the reply. **Who is he?**

Don't get nosy.

I should know who I'm scorching a path to Hell for with a pack of lies, slut. LOL.

Go back to your date.

Captain Kirk won't mind. He'll be on all night with commercial interruptions.

Marathon. BTW, Mike is looking for you. He sounded ticked.

When doesn't he?

He said it's been nearly a week. You can't avoid him forever. If he calls again, should I say you're in the shower?

In his case, you haven't heard from me, but you did hear there was an unidentified body somewhere in the next parish mangled on the railroad tracks.

Why the body gotta be mangled?

If you got hit by a train, what do you think your body would look like? It wouldn't be dapper don ready for a night of clubbing.

Hey, if you're busy getting busy, how are you texting me?

Brighton glanced at Gatien again. From the rise and fall of his shoulder, he could tell Gatien was asleep.

"Ass," he muttered to himself. Then he typed, **I'm not that busy. Nite.**

9

"HOLD STILL," Gatien ordered as he repositioned the cotton swab to insert more of the medicated gauze into the wound.

Brighton jerked again. "Then stop trying to break my arm."

"Quit bitching. You're not tender." Gatien finished packing the area, stepped back, and nodded. "There."

"Your bedside manner sucks," Brighton griped, staring at the bandaging. "And this looks like some Frankenstein meets The Mummy middle-of-the-battlefield shit."

"You planning on entering a beauty pageant? No? Then stop complaining. It's fine." He removed the latex gloves and discarded them in the trash. "Now do you want a blueberry, onion, or everything bagel?"

Brighton folded his arms, looked up with a discerning gaze, and jutted out his lips in a petulant pout. "Not hungry."

"Look, you, the instructions on this pill bottle say to take with food, so that's what you're going to do. Now what will it be: blueberry or everything?"

"What happened to onion?"

"I reconsidered. I don't want your onion breath in my face."

"I can take care of myself, you know."

"Dr. Jansen released you in my care. That means you do as I say."

Brighton's brows bunched together while the corners of his mouth turned downward. "You have serious control issues."

"Deal with it."

"I would if you give me my clothes from wherever you hid them. I'd go home."

"No, you wouldn't. You'd leave, think about it, and then go to a park or someplace. But you wouldn't go home."

"Why wouldn't I?"

Gatien shrugged. "I don't know. I'm not clairvoyant. You tell me."

"You seem to be reading tea leaves from somewhere."

"You want tea? I think I have some in the cabinet. If not, I can call the grocer back. I forgot to order milk when I got the bagels." He waved a pink sheet of paper that had been folded in one of the pharmacy bags. "It says here that milk is good for healing wounds."

"I'm not drinking milk."

"You're not, you're not, you're not." Gatien blew out a long breath. "Are you ever agreeable about anything?"

"Oh, you're one to talk. Don't even go there."

"Listen, Brighton, if you're going to be here for a couple of days—"

"I'm not staying here."

"—then we have to come to an understanding. You are going to follow these instructions, or I'm calling your doctor, and you can spend the rest of your recovery in a hospital room."

"It's a scratch!"

"Your doctor said it was severe enough to have killed you if it had been left untreated for much longer and that she had severe reservations about not admitting you. She said she had to cut out necr... nec... something tissue."

"Necrotizing."

"Yeah, that. She said she had to cut it out."

"Then problem solved. It's all gone."

"Don't be so flippant about your health."

"Oh, please. She pulled the death card scenario on you. But here's a secret. I'm not afraid of dying. No, living seems to be the more difficult thing to do."

"She said you'd say some bull like that."

Brighton's frown deepened. "Seems you two had quite the conversation."

"She cares. You don't see many physicians with that level of investment in their patients."

"She's been my doctor for a long time."

"I gathered that much. She said you never let on how sick you felt even when it was critical. What's that about?"

Sighing, Brighton stared out the window at the cloudless sky. "She shouldn't have told you that. It's a violation of HIPAA and my rights. I could sue her." He wouldn't, though—ever.

"Screw your rights. She was trying to be helpful."

"How? By billing me as some pathetic victim who requires your pity? Fuck that. I'm not a victim or a patsy."

Gatien tossed the paper on the nightstand and stormed toward the door. "You really are a piece of work. I'll be back with your bagel and juice."

"I don't want—"

The bedroom door slammed before Brighton completed his sentence. He groaned. *What is happening?*

Brighton climbed from the bed and pulled on the robe Gatien had draped across the bedpost. Standing, he felt a sluggishness he hadn't felt previously, and he placed his hand against the wall for balance as he made his way down the hallway to the kitchen.

Upon seeing him, Gatien glowered. "Dammit, what are you doing out of bed?"

Brighton flopped on a stool at the kitchen bar and leaned forward, breathing heavily. "Don't treat me like I'm sick. I can't stand when people do that."

"But you are sick."

His head snapped up and determination fired in his eyes as he emphasized each word. "I am not."

Gatien set the carton of apple juice on the counter, rounded the bar, and embraced Brighton from behind. "Hey. Calm down."

Brighton attempted to shrug Gatien off, but his hold was too firm. "I don't need your pity."

"No one is pitying you." He placed a feathery kiss atop Brighton's crown. "Trust me, you'd be hard-pressed to get an ounce of pity with your crabby behavior."

"Then why are you doing this?"

Gatien chuckled. "Because believe it or not, I like your little shit ass. But I need you to be straight with me. I don't like liars."

Brighton turned, stared into Gatien's eyes, and debated whether or not he wanted to step out on that proverbial limb and open the Pandora's crypt of foul. He weighed the rewards against the risks and considered if it was worth it. In a few short hours, life had become far more complicated. On the one hand, putting the cards on the table allowed for another hand to be dealt. Of course, it could also lead to getting shot, hypothetically speaking.

He drew in a deep breath he'd learned in the six hours of yoga he'd taken and counted to ten.

"When I was two," he began hesitantly, "my mom took me to Dr. Jansen for a fever. She diagnosed me with acute lymphoblastic leukemia."

"That's cancer, right?"

"Yeah. It took eight cycles of aggressive chemo, but I've been in remission for eighteen years."

"That's great."

Brighton shrugged. "I suppose. My mom became this nervous wreck. If I sniffed, she had me in a coffin. My father went into complete denial. When I lost my hair, he could barely stand to look at me. He avoided coming home as much as possible, and forget about him visiting me in the hospital. My siblings could never go anywhere or partici-pate in anything because someone always had to take care of me, be there for me. My being sick nearly tore my family apart. Then the cost of treatments left my family practically destitute, despite my father being an investment banker and my mother an accountant at a large law firm. They were forced to borrow money from my mother's half-brother, Mike Darbonne. They still haven't managed to repay it all."

Gatien released his grip and retreated. "The team's owner?"

"One of them. He owns a third."

"Michael Darbonne, the man who single-handedly is trying to fuck me over, is your uncle." It was more of an accusation than a question. "How convenient to have a nephew who can step right in and take my place at a frac-tion of the cost."

"See, I knew you would take it that way."

Gatien shook his head. "It's one thing to have a rival or competition after your job, but it's quite another to have it be indebted family. How do I compete with that? Son of a bitch," he muttered.

"I worked hard to get where I am, Gatien. But once the media finds out who I am, they'll react the same as you and say I'm only here because of nepotism."

Leaning against the cabinets, Gatien folded his arms across his powerful chest. "You're pretty good with those fancy words."

"The players will resent me; and the first off game I have, I'll be booted to the minors lickety-split." Brighton slipped from the stool. "I'll go. Give me my clothes."

"Now wait a minute." Gatien blocked Brighton's path. Snaking one arm around Brighton's waist, he flattened his palm against the younger man's back. His other hand tucked a lock of hair behind Brighton's ear, his knuckles brushing against his cheek before deliberately trailing his hand down Brighton's neck. The touch scoured a path on Brighton's skin to the hollow of his throat. "You're still in my care."

Brighton's body tingled at the touch as absurd and naughty thoughts plumed in his mind. His balls bunched in need in response to Gatien's teeth raking across his shoulders. He swallowed, his throat dry as he gazed into those simmering hazel eyes.

"I told you I can take care of myself."

"And I told you I like you. This just complicates things... a lot. Your uncle's business practices—"

"Are his. I don't want to talk about my uncle. I'm grateful to him, because I owe him my life. I can't ever repay that. So, I won't speak ill of him, but I'll be damned if I'm constantly in his shadow. It's unfortunate what's happening between you and him, but that's not my fault. You either see me as Brighton Rabalais or as Michael Darbonne's nephew."

"Fair enough." Gatien pressed his mouth back to Brighton's, that time firmer.

Conflicting emotions darted across Brighton's expressive face as the room's tension increased. The glimmer in his eyes warred between want and need. Brighton licked the seam of Gatien's mouth before permitting his tongue to dive deeper. Brighton tilted his chin, allowing Gatien's tongue to wrap against his in a heady, passionate duel—and teasing him with his tongue that urged for reciprocation. Granted, Brighton was relatively inexperienced, but no one had ever kissed him the way Gatien kissed him then, and Brighton feared he'd lose his mind. He couldn't will himself to pull away and not give in.

Through the denim, Brighton felt the hard length and thick ridge of Gatien's confined cock press and throb against his thigh. His own penis vaulted upright as excitement coursed through him.

"Are you sure you're feeling up for this?"

"Dammit, you left my balls clove-hitched last night. You either fuck me, or I swear I'll body slam and fuck the hell out of you."

"You would, wouldn't you? Okay, but not here," Gatien moaned into Brighton's mouth. The hedonistically raw gravel in Gatien's voice caused Brighton to shiver from his roots to toenails as the scruff on his jaws abraded Brighton's cheek.

Taking him by the hand, Gatien led him onto the glass-enclosed patio and guided him onto a wicker, padded bench, careful not to bump Brighton's bandaged elbow. He untied Brighton's robe, slipped it from his shoulders, and pushed him farther into the cushion.

"Let me get my hands on you," Brighton protested, pulling at the hem of Gatien's graphic T-shirt.

"Later."

"Now. I can't stand it."

Gatien nodded reluctantly. "Just for a moment." He fished his wallet out of his jeans and removed a condom and a sachet of lubricant. "Here," he said, handing the condom to the younger man. "Be quick about it. I can't wait. I want you," Gatien growled, unzipping his jeans and pushing them to his ankles.

Brighton smirked. *You'll wait all right.* He tore the corner from the foil and slowly rolled it down Gatien's length, tonguing every inch as he did. Once the latex reached the base, Brighton licked around the radius of Gatien's girth with a slick glide of his tongue, savoring the feel of him in his mouth before rubbing it with his nose and cheek.

As Gatien hoisted his shirt over his head, Brighton stood and planted chaste kisses on Gatien's chest before leaning into him and rubbing his nipples against the dense vault of muscle, each touch arousing and tense.

"Oh, that's good," Gatien cooed, then pushed Brighton back. "Enough. I want in." He squeezed the lube into his palm, stroked Brighton's crack, and then lathered his condom-sheathed erection. With his knee, he spread Brighton's asscheeks and brushed a finger around the tight rim before inserting a digit to his knuckle.

"Yes," Brighton huffed.

Gatien pushed his finger in further, slow and in a circular motion.

Brighton bit his lip and rocked back to meet Gatien's hand. "More," he demanded.

Gatien worked in another finger and scissored them.

"Stop teasing me. Take my ass."

"You love it." Laughing, Gatien worked his broad cockhead in the opening. Grunting as he pushed the head inside, he lowered himself to inches above Brighton.

Brighton relaxed beneath his heavy body. His breath caught as Gatien burrowed into him, pressing against every nerve ending that made a difference and withdrawing gradually until only his dome remained inside. The stretch was simultaneously soothing and chastening.

A skittish smile trembled on Brighton's lips for a second and then faded. White lights sparked behind his eyes as he stretched in a way he hadn't thought possible. Instinctively, his muscles squeezed the shaft with a hard contraction.

"Damn, you're tight. Early Merry Christmas to me."

"Again," Brighton pleaded, his breathing husky.

Gatien wasted no time increasing the rhythm, alternating long, deliberate strokes with short, quick ones. Each movement delved into Brighton's core and invaded his senses. Each twitch zinged in a new place that Brighton had no idea existed. He could wallow forever in the deliciousness of slick flesh sliding across flesh, the gentle breeze of the air conditioning skidding across his skin, the callouses on Gatien's broad hands scraping his back around to his collarbone. Brighton had not been with another man this way, but he knew he'd submit to Gatien whatever he requested.

Their rhythm grew savage and fearless. A barrage of meaningless vocalizations gurgled from Brighton's throat, indicating his building ecstasy. He was close. They both were.

Brighton fisted his penis and matched the speed of Gatien's thrusts. Gatien rocked his hips, arched his back, and craned his neck as his entire body locked. With a howl, his face strained as his climax detonated, taking Brighton crashing over the edge with him.

"Gatien," Brighton heaved. He wanted to say more, to express the sweeping tornado of emotions raging inside him, but the words evaded him. A bliss he'd never before felt churned inside him and stirred his blood. Although young and a lot inexperienced, he wasn't so naïve that he believed an afternoon of casual sex equated anything more than that. He also wasn't so green that he didn't understand that some heterosexual men, especially affluent adrenaline junkies who bored easily, got a charge from any controversial activity. The hell if he would walk around starry-eyed and delusional about proclamations of relationships. He knew the type of man he'd involved himself with.

Now get over it. That's what his head told him. Other areas became more complicated. It already felt more, different. Special. He had emotions blooming in him that he'd never experienced—or expected—ones he couldn't identify if his life depended upon it. And it almost felt as if his life *did* depend upon it by the way his heart thumped against his rib cage.

Gatien studied him. "You okay?"

"Perfect."

"Sorry. I should've taken it slower, eased you into it."

Brighton lowered his leg from the awkward position it was crooked in, becoming slightly self-conscious of how exposed he was. "Don't ruin it by apologizing. I'm not made of porcelain. I have two-hundred-pound men on skates trying to bulldoze me at twenty miles per hour."

"Only twenty? That's nothing. Just wait."

"What's the hardest hit you've ever taken?" He raked his fingers through his hair. "No, let me guess. The dirty hit from Bruno Kirkwood four years ago when he came off his feet and into the net from behind."

"That was pretty nasty," Gatien agreed. "But you'll find the most devastating hits occur off the ice."

10

"DUDE, THAT'S A FRIGGING CRATER," Semien stated, peering at Brighton's wound. "What did she use, an ice cream scoop?"

"I'm sure it was a basic run-of-the-mill scalpel."

"I hope you got it on video. That baby must've been something awesome to see split open."

Brighton laughed, shook his head, and replaced the gauze over his incision. "You're one sick individual."

Semien laughed and stood from the couch in the center of his high-rise loft that overlooked the city. "You want a beer?"

"Sure, why not? I've been off the sauce for five days. I'm due a cold one."

Semien glanced over his shoulder from the refrigerator. "So, where were you hiding the last week, hooka?"

"Don't start that."

"Ah, not kissing and telling, huh?" Semien grabbed two beers and returned to the couch.

"You wouldn't believe me if I told you."

Semien handed Brighton a beer, twisted the cap off his, and flopped onto the sofa. "Try me."

Brighton sipped his beer and held up the bottle. "Since when did you start drinking import?"

"Nicco turned me on to it at his Fourth of July barbecue. He's in a beer-of-the-month club. Come to think of it, he's in a lot of 'of-the-month' clubs—whiskey, pie, bacon, wine, coffee, cheese, celery sticks, condoms... and don't think I didn't catch you changing the subject." He stretched. "I know I haven't been around much the last year since signing and all, but you're my boy. You know you can confide in me."

"Yeah, I know, but I don't know how to explain it."

"Dude, it's not painting the Sistine Chapel."

"Do you even know where that is?"

"Getting snarky won't change any facts."

"Part of me is afraid to talk about it. I don't want to jinx it. The other part of me doesn't know what to say. Is it real? Hell, I don't know. Yet the other part of me, the smarter part, says I shouldn't talk about it because it can create issues I don't need in my life right now. Another part—"

"Dang, how many parts of you are there?"

Brighton chuckled. "More than enough to be useless."

"Well, there's no need to confess your wicked ways to me, but just so you know, your cover is blown. Mike's been by several times. He knows you haven't been here."

"I figured as much."

"That roommate of yours narced on you. I think he did it for revenge because he's ticked at you for not going back to your place." Semien took a swallow of beer and relaxed into the cushions of the couch. "What's his deal, anyway? He wouldn't have ever been someone you would've hung around with when I was there."

Brighton shrugged. "He seemed like he could use a friend. I met him at a stockcar race rally to support purchasing a live mascot. He was trying to get the attention of one of the drivers, and I felt sorry for him the way the guy blew him off. I know he's a bit socially awkward—"

"Dude, sociopaths have better social skills. I wasn't with him five minutes, and I wanted to ram my stick down his throat."

"Careful," Brighton replied with a smirk, "he might like that."

Semien nudged Brighton's calf with his foot. "My hockey stick. You know what I meant. But I'm going to be the least of his problems if Aidan catches him making goo-goo eyes at Christophe. Now tell me what's been going on with you this week. You've gone and caught feelings?"

"I might've, but it's not something I expect to pan out."

"Why not?"

"Because he's not gay."

"Wait a minute. Rewind. What?"

"At best, he's bi."

"What do you mean, at best?"

"It's more one of those prison wolf things where he jumps what's available."

Semien choked on his beer. "You've been holed up with a convict?"

"No, goofball. He's an extreme sportster, the kind of person who requires high-stakes adventure. I imagine undercover freaking with the other team is on his bucket list of what he can get away with without getting caught."

"And you know this because...?"

"He's got a long history of radical behavior—base jumping, street luge, white water rafting, paragliding, mountain climbing—and a longer list of girlfriends. Zen isn't his thing, unless it involves a volcano and a surfboard."

"Why would you involve yourself with someone like that? You're usually so level-headed and... prudish."

Brighton grimaced. "I'm no prude."

"Ha! You're Admiral Fuddy-duddy. Skipping flossing for a day is a trek on the wild side for you. And heaven forbid the floss be flavored."

"Gum disease runs in my family, and I don't know why I did it. I'll admit, I may have gotten swept away in the moment, in the delusion of a possibility from him feeding me croissants, crumpets, and crêpes stuffed with mascarpone in bed. But as I said, at the end of the day, I was a person of convenience. And if you don't buy any of that, I can always fall back on the fact that I had a fever—a very high one."

Semien grunted. "I've seen you play shutouts without allowing a fever to get in your way. Panhandle that hullabaloo somewhere else to someone who didn't drink the cherry Kool-Aid."

"Why is it always cherry and never grape or strawberry?"

"Cherry's the best."

"Well, now's not a good time for me to be starting a relationship anyway. I need to focus on my career."

"Unless you're planning on snuggling with a biscuit at night, a career with no one in it won't be fulfilling."

"So says the kettle."

"I date."

"No, you don't. You hook up. Big difference."

"Because women see me as a meal ticket and baby daddy. All they want is red carpet events and bling. When I pulled my hamstring and had to sit out four games and rumor got out I wouldn't be returning, they all disappeared fast. No one came to feed me crumpets with macaroni in bed."

"Mascarpone. And it was stuffed crêpes."

"That, too. But this isn't about me. And even if it was, I've never invented such pathetic excuses as the ones you just gave. If you're going to spew malarkey, you could at least be creative. For once, why don't you try more than just surviving and live a little? Get your mom out of your head."

"She's not in my head."

"Oh yes, she is— jabbing you with a searing cerebral pitchfork. There's no other reason why you didn't enter the draft when I did than your mom."

"She wanted me to get a degree."

"She wanted you not to play hockey, to be a sheltered, monotonous accountant like her."

"What's wrong with being able to do my own taxes? It's a noble profession."

"Who says it's not? But it's also one that tucks you in a safe corner where the big bad boys don't hit you. It's the same reason you don't cut your hair." Semien took another sip of beer and crossed his ankle atop his knee. "Know what I think?" He tore open a bag of potato chips and popped one in his mouth.

"Nope, but I'm sure you're about to proclaim the gospel according to Semien."

"I think you're drawn to this guy, whoever he is, because he is the risk taker, because he's spontaneous and unpredictable. In fact, I think that's the reason you've shacked up with that dude you call a roommate—not because you like him, but because he's outlandish in a way you don't allow yourself to be. You went for someone who's unobtainable so it wouldn't work out. That way you don't actually have to deal with anything and can stay in that protected, sequestered world you've carved for yourself with the added bonus that your parents don't have to accept you being gay. They can continue denying and pretending the way they do with everything else concerning you."

"Damn you, Semy." Brighton exhaled a harsh breath as if he'd been walloped in the gut. He hated that his friend knew him so well. "Psychology would've been the only class you paid attention in. Why couldn't you have skipped it like you did all the rest?"

"Just calling them like I see them, bruh."

"Then stop looking. It's annoying."

"Getting back to this mascarpone. Isn't that the gobbledygook women used on their eyelashes?"

MAYBE SEMIEN HAS A POINT.
The conversation he'd had with his bestie weighed heavily on his mind as he strolled through the business district to the executive offices of Whittle, Darbonne, & Shaw. He'd walked those sidewalks hundreds of times, but the magnificence of the skyscrapers breaching the heavens never failed to impress. Their mirrored windows reflected the sun and cast a golden glow on the congested streets. The view almost lifted the dread of having to meet with his uncle.

The two had agreed to meet for lunch, but Brighton's follow-up doctor's appointment had been bumped up an hour due to a cancellation. Brighton figured he could take advantage of the situation by meeting with his uncle at the downtown office instead of a restaurant, where he was sure Mike would've reserved a private room. Private dining would constitute having to wait for their meals, which Brighton anticipated his uncle would instruct to be delayed in serving. Showing up unannounced would reduce the length of the meeting and the amount of time he'd have to spend listening to how much he owed the franchise.

In the large print, his signing bonus was great. But in the fine print, he'd agreed to relinquish 15 percent of his salary as repayment for medical bills, as well as allowing his uncle to manage him. That meant an additional 15 percent going to Mike. Brighton viewed it as a small price to pay; however, he could do without the lectures and guilt trips to keep him in line.

In his jeans and red cotton pull-over, he stuck out amongst the gray designer suits and beige trouser sets littering the building's lobby. Because security was used to seeing him, he breezed through the check-in and visitor passes.

The rushing clicks of heels against the slate floor echoed in the corridor. He fell into step and took the elevator to the twenty-ninth floor.

A door banged open when he stepped off the elevator, and his aunt Verna emerged carrying a large box mummi-fied in bubble wrap and shipping tape. Brighton rushed over to help.

"Here, let me get that, Auntie," he told her, lifting the burdensome box from her petite arms that barely encircled it.

"Thank you, sweetie, but you don't need to."

"No problem. Where's it go?"

"To the conference room."

"This is heavy. You shouldn't be carrying this in your state."

"Honey, I've been doing this job since long before you

were born and through all of my pregnancies. But it's very thoughtful of you."

He stared at her very round belly and smiled, wondering how many of his six previous unborn cousins were due to his aunt's extraneous lifting work duties. This was the furthest he'd ever seen her.

"After all this time, don't you think you've warranted a promotion from the mailroom to a desk job?" *Or better yet, as a stay-at-home socialite.* It was no secret that Mike Darbonne's success was largely due to his wife and her working to pay for his college education.

"Oh, I'd just make a mess of things anyplace else. I don't have a head for numbers like your mother, and I think other executives might find it a bit awkward to have a partner's wife as an administrative assistant. Besides, this is where Mike needs me." She smiled sweetly. "He needs someone to ensure deliveries are properly received and logged." She tapped the box. "These are the prototypes for the new helmets to keep you boys safe. It incorporates a new impact-absorbing foam."

"Still, Auntie...." He tapered off when he saw Verna's gaze drop. The last thing he wanted was to make her feel inferior or like any of the miscarriages had been her fault. "Fault me for being a chauvinist, but as long as I'm around, you won't be carrying heavy boxes."

"Verna," Amy from packing called in her thick Haitian accent, rushing down the hall. "Mr. Taniguchi from Tokyo is calling, and he sounds in a right state. He insists on speaking only with you."

"And I have a few words for him," Verna replied, stopping in her tracks. "All the wire facemasks were packed inadequately and corroded during shipping. He's in for a rude awakening if he thinks we're accepting those things."

She refocused on Brighton. "Take that down and set it on the table for me, sweetie. I'll be there after I deal with Mr. Tan-think-again-guchi."

He chuckled at her sass. "Sic 'em, Auntie."

Readjusting the box, he continued down the corridor toward the conference rooms and then paused. Since the contents of the box he carried were prototypes, Brighton took a gamble that his aunt would want to unload it in the private conference room instead of the one with the glass walls. Besides, it was farther down the corridor, and he welcomed any excuse that prolonged meeting with his uncle.

As he approached the conference room, he slowed at the sound of voices.

"You've always been predictable in the most unusual ways," a male voice said. "I remember in the game against Texas, the clapper that came barreling at 102 miles per hour into that beautiful, broad breadbasket of yours with four minutes left in the third, you slapping it down like it was merely an inconvenience, and then skating it end-to-end for a goal you knew wouldn't count. I took one look at you tracking that biscuit slicing through the air and knew you were bored with the game. You just said 'screw it, fuck getting a penalty, I'm gonna do what I wanna do, I'm going to get my jollies.'"

Brighton recognized the voice. *Mike.*

"That's what makes you an amazing player who's fascinating to watch, that spunk and spontaneity," Mike continued. "Your charisma captures the passion and contagious enthusiasm of the crowd—even that of the opposing team. No one knows what exactly you're going to do, but everyone knows you're going to do something unorthodox—something... scintillating."

"Don't act like you know me."

Gatien.

"But I do." Ruthlessness meshed with Mike's natural gravelly intonation in a roguish and disturbing combination. "Just as I knew my nephew would crawl under your skin like a tasty morsel, but I had no idea it would be so quick with that temper of yours. Then again, you could never stay angry long, could you?"

What the hell?

A phone rang, followed by shuffling and a thump as if something had fallen to the floor.

"Back off me, Mike."

"Darla!" Mike growled. "I told you not to have contact with that bitch anymore. It's over between the two of you, do you hear me? You've nothing left to say to her."

Metal scraped against the floor as if something had been pushed.

"You don't get to make that decision." Gatien hissed. "Give me back my fucking phone."

"But I do. You're mine. I have you under contract. And even if I didn't, you'd still be mine. I own you."

"You don't own shit."

"Your mouth is so succulent when you're angry. All the naughty things you do with it."

Dafuq! Brighton rounded the doorjamb and glowered at the sight of Gatien reclined on the table with Mike atop of him, cramming his tongue into Gatien's mouth and tugging at Gatien's trousers.

"Son-of-a-bitch," Brighton snapped. "Both of you." He threw the box in the couple's direction and exited, his long strides taking him quickly down the corridor to the elevators.

"Wait!" Gatien called as the elevator door closed with Brighton inside.

By the time Brighton made it to the lobby, tears stung in his eyes. *What's wrong with me? Through all the years of chemo, I never once shed a tear. Now, over a fling, the waterworks turn on?*

"No!" He willed himself to stop crying, swiping at his eyes. He would not do this.

He stepped out of the elevator, exited the building, and rejoined the real world—abandoning the fantasy universe he had started constructing in his head over the past week.

What a shitbasket.

11

BRIGHTON RECLINED on the bench in the cool interior of the reptile house, evading the sun and heat—among other things. As a child, his parents frequently brought him to the Saint Anne Zoo between chemo cycles and spent hours marveling at giraffes that spat, elephants that stank, and zebras that pooped while they walked. Over time, the zoo had transformed into his safe place when life seemed to close in on him.

The animals were his kindred spirits—trapped inside cages, longing to roam free while watching the outside world scuttle by gleefully. The younger him had been trapped by poisons in his body that consisted of cells, tumors, chemicals, and vicious fears that the torture would never cease. The anticipation of what laid in the future and the waiting were worse than the actual experience of being ill. But they were nothing compared to the ache he now felt in his heart.

His poor aunt. How could he tell her that the man she hung the heavens on was no greater than the speckled green flecks on goose crap? She wouldn't be able to handle it, and the stress could send her into premature labor. Did he want that bearing on his soul? Plus, the child... Mike didn't deserve to be a father, to be given an opportunity to corrupt and maim an innocent. However, not telling Verna seemed deceitful despite the risk. Then again, maybe his aunt was one of those women who wouldn't want to know the truth about her husband, one who preferred to live a life of denial.

Or perhaps he overthought the situation and gave himself too much credit. What if the real reason he wanted to blab to Verna was to stick it to Mike—provided Mike cared and had feelings to be hurt? Mike, of course, would care if Verna sued him for divorce, alimony, and child support in a state that guaranteed her 50 percent of the marital assets. She could prune him to his knees to pay for all his sins. Well, probably not all of them, because Brighton imagined that list to be extensive. But Verna was a proud woman, and Brighton knew she'd never do such a thing.

Eyes still burning from tears, he glanced at the screen of his vibrating phone. Gatien again. Nine times—not that Brighton was counting—Gatien had called since Brighton left the firm. He didn't bother swiping to decline, allowing the call to go to voice mail. Gatien meant nothing to him. He refused to allow him to mean anything. No, Gatien wasn't the reason Brighton wanted to do nothing more than curl into a fetal position and stare at the darkness. He was nothing more than a hookup. People did it all the time. Granted, Brighton never had, but that was beside the point.

"Fuck!" he muttered. He had to work with these people. Sighing, he pushed his hair over his shoulders, watched a reticulated python slither along the glass, and grunted at the irony. He'd traded one set of snakes for another, and, frankly, he'd preferred to keep company with the legless one. "Bitch asses."

Brighton's cell vibrated again, and he read the name of the car dealership. *Finally.* He could use some good news to pull him out of—or at least momentarily distract him from—this funk. It had been nearly three weeks since he'd filed the warranty claim for his car. He'd been told it would only take a couple of days—clearly not the case.

He answered and listened as the mechanic delved into an extended litany of car engine decompression, octane, and blah, blah, blah, during which the only words Brighton understood were "not covered by warranty."

"My warranty is five years. I've only had the car for eighteen months."

"Yes, sir, but as I explained, the warranty is voided when proper maintenance isn't maintained."

"What are you talking about? I bring it in to be serviced at your dealership every three thousand miles. Check your records."

"But you've also been using a nitrous oxide agent."

"What does what I do in my dentist office have to do with my car? I didn't wreck while high."

"In your engine, sir."

"What in my engine?"

"The nitrous oxide."

"Why would I put laughing gas in my engine? It doesn't need a root canal. More importantly, how? I don't have some nitrous oxide lab in my home or cook the stuff up on my kitchen stove."

"It's poured or pumped into the gas tank."

"You saying I got a batch of bad gas?"

"Doubtful at these levels. Your pistons are all blown. That indicates extensive use. Unless you're using a station with unregulated octane—which is unlikely—this would not be fuel from a corner gas pump."

Clenching his jaw, Brighton massaged his temple to relieve the forming headache. His two plus two wasn't equaling four.

After a beat of silence, the mechanic asked, "You don't understand, do you?"

"Not jack other than the dealership trying to weasel out of its warranty obligation and this sounding like a shitload of money about to come out of my pocket."

"Mr. Rabalais, nitrous oxide is used in racing cars to enhance performance. Not all cars are built to use that type of fuel, and special conversion fueling systems are necessary."

"I don't race. In fact, I rarely drive. I let my roommate borrow it more than I dr...." The words died on Brighton's lips.

Dylan. Could he have done this? Surely if he had, he would've said something. Wouldn't he?

He watched as another python camouflaged by the aquarium foliage uncoiled in a corner and flickered its forked tongue. Yep, snakes hiding everywhere—even in plain sight.

THE FRONT DOOR to Brighton's townhouse shut louder than he'd anticipated, making him aware that he hadn't cooled off much since leaving the zoo. He'd stayed at the zoo so long that the chimpanzees had all gathered in a tree, staring at him as if he were the attraction, and he'd begun to understand their language. He still would've been there, lost in the passage of time, had the zoo staff not ushered him out for closing. Why he'd come home instead of stopping at a bar to mull over an unwanted drink puzzled him, since home was the last place he wanted to be. Actually, the last place he wanted to be was around people. He didn't mind being at home alone, but he knew Dylan was there.

And speaking of the devil, Dylan stepped into the living room and crossed his arms staunchly across his narrow chest. His nostrils flared. "Well, look who decided to come home and grace this humble abode with his almighty presence."

"I don't have to check in with you."

"Five days and you couldn't phone more than once? Answer my calls? Let me know you weren't dead in a ditch?"

"You knew I wasn't."

"Oh, right. Because you were with your *bff*, Semy, who hasn't been around for the past year." The veins in his face constricted. "But we both know that's a lie. So, where were you?"

"You're not my boyfriend. You don't get to ask me that question."

Dylan's mouth gaped. "What? You finally get some dick and this is how I'm treated? I've done nothing but be there for you, and you have the audacity to say that to me?"

"Audacity? This coming from the person who blew up my car?"

Dylan's eyes widened.

"Yeah, I know all about it. Why'd you do it? To impress that drag racer guy who wouldn't give you the time of day? What was his name again, Rick? Did it at least get you laid?"

"I know your closeted ass isn't trying to slut-shame me."

"I've never been in the closet, but I don't feel the need

to run down the street with a rainbow banner, either. My sexuality is a part of me. It doesn't define me."

"Please! Save it for the peanut gallery. You don't want all your new hockey buddies knowing you catch for the other team."

"For your information, the first person I came out to was Semien, and he's never cared or judged. Second, the guys on the team aren't going to give a rat's ass about what the nobody rookie backup goalie does off the ice. But mostly, I'm a hockey player who happens to be gay, not a gay hockey player. Who are you?"

"The person who loves you."

Brighton tossed his head back, cackled, and shook his head. Nothing about Dylan's statement sounded remotely genuine.

"You don't love me. You don't even know me."

"I live with you."

"So? You have no clue what it is I do on the ice, what it's like when you call my mother about something trivial going on with me, why I choose to avoid Mike—nothing. I've been with Gatien for less than a week, and he knows more about me."

"Gatien?" Dylan's face dropped. "That's who you've been fucking? The guy who makes you almost piss your pants each time his name is mentioned? I never took you for someone who would sleep his way to the top of the hockey world, especially since you have your uncle."

Brighton threw up his hand. "I'm not discussing this with you, Dylan. This conversation is over. Now excuse me while I go figure out how I'm going to pay for my car repairs and the rent."

"Bri—"

"Stay away from me. I've had enough. My head is spinning, and I don't want to see your face right now."

Brighton stormed to his room, slamming the door behind him—intentionally. Tears continued to prick the corners of his eyes, but sheer stubbornness kept them at bay. He sank into an ornate leather armchair, lowered his head into his palms, and rested his elbows on his knees. His knuckles whitened and his palms sweated, his body shuddering with each breath as he attempted to make sense of what had transpired.

How was it possible? It had taken him three years to beat cancer, four years to get a degree, sixteen years to make it from mite hockey to pro, and less than two minutes to have his entire life destroyed. Dr. Jansen had labeled him as a fighter, but any fight remaining in him had drained away.

What had he expected? Some long, happy future with a white picket fence, brick house, bushy-tailed dog, and two-point-five children? Hell, that didn't even happen in fairy tales anymore.

He released a long breath. His knight in shining armor has a spit-polish finish, glowing surface, and a shitload of problems beneath.

12

"I WAS THINKING MORE OLD-SCHOOL," Brighton explained to Diane. "Clean lines, monochromatic, and a big logo."

"You could do that," the artist replied, her voice lagging in enthusiasm.

"You think it's a shitty choice?"

"Listen, it's your helmet. You're the one wearing it. I'm here to make you happy."

"You're also commissioned to make me look good. Your opinion matters."

"What about doing a nickname in graffiti lettering on the backplate? What do your teammates call you?"

Brighton's face contorted at the thought of having "poo boo" scripted in metallic gold lettering on his helmet for all the world to see. *Fuck no.* "What else you got?"

"You could do a superhero motif, or maybe an alien civet with laser beams shooting from its eyes."

"Or I could have claw marks."

"I think that's a bit boring and not much of a statement for a freshman goalie."

"That's sort of the point, to be understated. I don't want to come off as some arrogant noob."

She waved her hands as if swatting an insect. "All the more reason to go bold. You want the fans to be wowed the first time you take the ice. It's like getting your V-card stamped. It needs to be memorable. The mask is your face for sixty minutes."

"I'm backup. No way do I get sixty minutes of play."

"It doesn't matter if it's sixty seconds. You still want the crowd to be blown away when they flash your closeup on the Jumbotron. Besides, this is your first custom helmet. You should have fun with it."

"She's right, you know," Gatien said from the doorway.

Brighton groaned. "What's he doing here?"

"You're not the only goalie in town. Diane's been doing my artwork for years."

"Figures," Brighton muttered. Not only had he been tickled by the fickle finger of fate to be screwing the same man as his uncle, but they also shared a helmet artist. *So much for supporting local businesses.* He slipped off the stool and faced Diane. "Let me sleep on it, and I'll call you tomorrow." Not that he would be able to sleep any.

"Brighton, we should talk," Gatien called out.

"No, thanks." He exited the studio, and Gatien followed. "I've crossed enough items off the shitty-things-that-can-happen-to-me-this-week list."

"You need to listen."

His headache hadn't faded. Piling Gatien atop everything else going on wasn't going to happen. Not today. Not if Brighton could help it.

"I'm busy." He whipped out his cell and checked the time, although he knew he was way ahead of schedule. He'd blocked two hours for the graphic artist, but he'd only spent forty-five minutes meeting with her. His photo shoot for "everyday" pictures to update and overhaul what would now be his official social media page wasn't for another three hours. As Heather, the head public relations representative for the Civets, had explained, Brighton didn't have a large enough following yet to require a website, and until he did, his personal social media pages would have to serve in its place. That required professionals to orchestrate and contrive his appearing ordinary and spontaneous, which included taking photos with a dog he didn't own and on a jet ski in a studio pool with friends he'd never met and a fan blowing his hair—events that gave an accurate depiction of his day-to-day life. *Yeah, okay.*

"I don't have the patience for you being obstinate today," Gatien grumbled.

Brighton increased his stride and turned onto Mag Avenue, where his favorite creamery was located. Screw an apple a day keeping the doctor away. A scoop of Mississippi mud and rocky road mixed on a slab would force Gatien to keep his trap shut. He couldn't very well talk with something in his lusciously plump mouth.

What roguish things that mouth could do....

And now also wasn't the time for some awkward boner, though Brighton was well on his way to getting there. *Focus!* He was supposed to be pissed. No, he *was* pissed—not exactly cut-a-bitch pissed, but pretty damn close—and he refused to be sidetracked by his treacherous libido that threatened to rip through his zipper.

Brighton hurried into the creamery and asked the lady waiting in line if he could skip her. She agreed with a flirty smile wasted on him, and he ordered two waffle cones. Even if he wasn't gay, the pink curlers in her hair weren't a look that would've revved his engine.

Engine... another topic he'd like to avoid.

"What are you doing?" Gatien asked.

The question triggered a joke setup response: a man walks into an ice cream parlor.... But Brighton refrained. He wasn't in a joking mood. "Getting ice cream." *I scream, you scream, we all scream for ice cream. But all I want to do is scream at you until your ears bleed and you hurt and feel as shitty as I do. No... worse.* He looked back to the pock-faced teen server. "Make those double scoops."

At this rate, he'd be a gelato and soft serve basehead by the time he got the veteran goalie out of his system—although Gatien never served up anything soft.

Stop!

He leaned against the glass enclosure, allowing the coolness to seep into his skin.

The server was quick and handed the cones to Brighton. He accepted, passed one to Gatien, paid, and then exited to the street again.

Gatien stepped in front of him. "Brighton—"

"Your ice cream is melting."

"So, let it. You and I need to talk."

"I don't want to talk to you."

"Then listen."

"I don't want to do that, either." He stepped around Gatien and crossed to the neutral ground.

"That's too damn bad." He grabbed Brighton's upper arm and pulled him to a halt long enough for the loading streetcar to fill to capacity.

"You ass!" Brighton complained.

"We've covered that before. Now listen to me."

"I will not. I don't listen to liars. All your self-righteous bull about truth and honesty. *Pfft.*"

"I never lied to you."

"No? You're fucking my uncle. My *married* uncle. How could you do that?" He turned to leave but pirouetted instead. "You bastard! That's like one step away from incest for me. Gross!"

"I'm—"

"I mean, I knew he was using me for bait, and that you considered me some piece of fly-by-night hot ass, but I never dreamed I'd be a bargaining chip between the two of you, some useless slab of meat."

"It wasn't like that."

"It isn't even about me. If you knew all the things my aunt has gone through for him and what a good woman she is, you'd understand just how completely shitty this is."

"You have it all wrong."

"I don't think so. But even if I did, you looked me in the eye and denied having an affair with Darla Richards."

"Because I didn't."

"I heard what my uncle said."

"What *he* said. But you haven't heard what *I* have to say."

"There's nothing you can say that would change anything."

"He was blackmailing me."

"And you chose money over people." He pulled away and began walking toward a cluster of trees.

"You're wrong. I chose people over self-respect, which is the most foolish decision ever. People are bad investments, and they never fail to let you down. You're no different."

Brighton froze. "What?"

"You're determined to close me out. This is just an excuse. You never wanted to hear the truth, even when I tried to tell you. You said you wouldn't discuss your uncle. It's what you do, Brighton. You run away from people."

"I've never run away from anything in my life."

"I didn't say thing. I said people. You run from people, avoid confrontation—which is quite odd for a goalie. Then again, most goalies are out of the action until they're confronted."

"Our job is to stay in position and defend the net, not skate to center ice and tackle defensemen." A feat Gatien had been known to do a time or two.

"Because you're complacent to only fight battles directly in front of you. You cover the puck and kill the play, but if there's something worth fighting for that means you have to move from the blue, forget it. You don't knock it out to your forward to have him take it down for a chance to score. Instead, you take the chickenshit way out."

Brighton heaved and took a step closer to Gatien. "Okay, I'm listening."

Bystanders were staring at them. Gatien pointed to a vacant streetcar bench farther down the neutral area. "Let's sit over there."

"Fine."

The two strolled to the covered seating and situated themselves.

"So, tell me." Brighton licked dripping ice cream from his hand.

Gatien released a shaky breath. "Now that we're here, I hardly know where to begin."

"The beginning would be nice."

"I was born on a Sunday."

"If you're not going to be serious—" Brighton started to stand.

"Okay, okay. But this isn't the easiest for me."

Brighton noted the genuineness in Gatien's voice and

nodded. "The first words are usually the hardest. I find blurting things out works well."

"Well, not this time. You need to hear the entire story." Gatien paused and glanced toward the sky before continuing. "I met Darla on a hiking expedition several years ago through Unlimited Adventure Huntsmen. It's a private club that arranges extreme excursions. She and I hit it off right away."

"See? You said you weren't involved with her."

"Not the way you think. I never said we weren't friends. If you'd listen, I'll explain."

"Okay," Brighton muttered, biting into his waffle cone.

"Darla used to work as a real estate agent. One day, she was showing a house in a remote area when a plane flying over decided to dump the excrement from its waste holding tank. It crashed through the roof like a bomb, and part of the ceiling fell on Darla. She was hospitalized for months with a fractured spine. Doctors said she'd never walk again."

"But she seems to walk fine on the show."

"She does now, but it took her a long time to get there— years of physical therapy, overcoming an addiction to prescription pain pills, and so on. One day, she had enough and said she wanted to change her life, so she joined UAH. The thing about UAH is that most people who join do so with a partner because there're lots of couple events, like dances after the main adventure to celebrate. She didn't have one, and neither did I. It seemed natural—"

"That the two of you become a couple. I get it."

"No, you don't. We became excursion partners, not a couple. When she started doing *MotoCaid*, the media picked up a romantic angle. There was never anything between us other than friendship—strictly platonic."

"If that were the case, why didn't either of you ever

correct it? And why would Mike insist that you have nothing to do with her?"

"Because I was in a relationship."

"You just said there was nothing between you and Darla."

"Not with Darla. With Harper."

The waffle cone tumbled from Brighton's hand onto the grass. He whipped his head around as if he'd been bitch-slapped. "What?"

"When I met Harper Kincaid, he was dating Darla, but there was an instant spark between him and me. At first, we tried to ignore it, but it kept growing. Harper wanted to keep it a secret, but I couldn't, especially since Darla confided in me that she was developing feelings for Harper but felt she was doing something to turn him off."

"You told her?"

"Of course."

"How'd she take it?"

"Not well at first, but she came around. Only Harper didn't. By then, writers had started scripting a relationship between him and Darla in the show. He said it would kill the ratings if viewers learned the truth." Gatien chuckled but not in amusement. "I stupidly believed it was all about the show like he said. But the truth was he didn't want to come out. And for him not to be outed meant my staying in as well."

"So, you really are gay?"

"You couldn't figure that out? I thought I made it pretty clear."

"I... I... you were always with so many women."

"And? I have four sisters and tons of female friends. My agent is a woman, and so is her assistant, not to mention my barber, dry cleaner, and insurance agent.

Since when is a gay man not allowed to be seen with women?"

"I didn't mean it that way." Brighton folded his hands in his lap. "How did my uncle get involved?"

"Harper's a member of UAH, too. That's where he and Darla met. At the time, he was a gold member, and that's why he and I didn't cross paths for a long time. Darla and I both started at platinum level. But Harper's thing is more indoor sports, if you get my drift. He likes being in spaces that are risqué."

"Public sex?"

"Well, public places. The thing is, when you sign up for an excursion, you accept that there're certain associate risks. And should those risks occur, you must be willing to accept the consequences. Harper has an invincibility complex, that the bad will never happen to him."

"So, what happened?"

"He wanted to go to the arena, to visit the restricted areas. I took him to the announcement booth, and he got turned on. We both did. He wanted to watch us go at it on the Jumbotron. Michael was in one of the private boxes and saw everything. The next day, he called me to his office and said if I didn't do what he asked, he'd feed the story to the media. I told him to go ahead, but when Harper found out, he begged me to meet Michael's demands. I thought it would be a onetime deal, but blackmailers keep coming back for more. Finally, Michael demanded that I end things with Harper."

"Why didn't you dispute the relationship with the media, say it wasn't true? No one would've believed it."

"I didn't want to. Why should I have to hide who I am? I was supposed to be Harper's boyfriend, not some soiled toilet paper." He lifted his chin. "Plus, Michael had it all on video, recorded it on his phone. When I initially refused his demands, he went straight to Harper, convinced him to relocate the filming locale to Atlanta." He clicked his tongue. "Michael feasted on Harper's fear of the truth tanking the show and his career. Darla would become collateral damage. And Michael believes when I talk with Darla that it's my way of sneaking off with Harper."

Brighton's voice dropped. "You cared for Harper, didn't you?"

"Once. He was my weakness, but that was before I realized I could never be first in his life. Do you know how hard it is to compete with reality television?"

Brighton shook his head. "I can't imagine."

"I ended things with Harper a year ago, and it had nothing to do with the blackmail. I told Michael I wouldn't sleep with him again, either. That's when he started the bullshit about my contract."

"I'm so sorry, Gatien."

"Why are you apologizing? It's Michael's doing, not yours."

"I know, but I feel bad."

"You and your Catholic guilt. You shouldn't. I fell for the wrong person back then." He reached across, took Brighton's hands in his, and rubbed his thumb across his knuckles. "But now I see someone I'd like to start something with."

"You can't let my uncle get away with this." Brighton's soulful eyes hooked Gatien's.

"He already has. It isn't about me. I don't care who knows I'm gay. I don't even care that much about Harper losing his TV show. But Darla doesn't deserve the shrapnel. She'll be publicly humiliated that her entire relationship has been a farce, branded as a reality star whore who maintained an elaborate lie for cash. Her real estate business will suffer, and in this economy, it's already bad enough. Then there's your aunt to consider."

"So... what? You're going to continue sleeping with Mike until he's too old to get it up?"

Gatien gazed into Brighton's concerned eyes. "No. That's done."

"How can you be so sure?" Brighton's brows quirked. "You said it yourself that he keeps coming back."

"It's best that you don't know."

"I thought we were being honest with each other."

"I hired someone to... investigate." He mumbled the word, and his lips curled in self-contempt. "You know ... look into his records."

"You hacked him."

"Well, not me personally, and I can't be 100 percent positive how the information was acquired since I wasn't there." He waggled his eyebrows.

"Uh-huh."

"I hired my investigator several months back, but I received the results two days ago. Your uncle buried things pretty deep."

Brighton constricted his mouth. "What did your *investigation* find?"

"It looks as if Michael may have embezzled from the franchise."

"No way! How much?"

"It's hard to determine an exact amount because it extends for years, but it seems to be seven figures."

"Holy shit!" Brighton's jaw dropped, and he was speechless for several moments. "And you're sure about this?"

"The evidence seems compelling. I confronted him

with it today, right after you left. The deal is: he keeps quiet, I keep quiet."

Staring at the ground, Brighton shoved his trembling fingers through his hair, uncertain of what to say next. But he knew this conversation wasn't over.

13

BRIGHTON STARED at the grass and concrete. Like the ice cream splattered there, the emotions swirling in him felt like wasted energy. This man before him made him feel emotions he'd never felt and stole his breath in ways that made breathing seem unnecessary. Yet it was all too soon and new. How could he have fallen so hard so quickly? Was that even possible?

At Thanksgiving, when the family had all gathered for dinner and were required to state what they were thankful for, his father always mentioned how he'd fallen in love with his wife the first time he saw her. He'd been a young courier for an advertising company at the time, working his way through college, and she'd been depositing coins in a parking meter across the street from his first delivery of the day. Brighton adored the story of his father almost being plowed over on his ten-speed by a yellow commuter bus while cutting across traffic to meet the mystery woman wearing retro go-go boots and a bubblegum-pink minidress.

Brighton especially enjoyed the way his father became lost in the words as if reliving the moment, all other family members at the table momentarily vanishing. All those times listening, Brighton assumed that was simply something all married couples did. But now he questioned if there was more to it. In Gatien's presence, the rest of the world faded to blurs, blobs, and all other kinds of inconsequential contours that failed to make sense. Brighton got that same goofy look of euphoria when thinking of Gatien as his father did at Thanksgiving dinner.

"Hey." Gatien nudged Brighton's foot with his own. A light breeze carried the scent of beignets. "The streetcar is coming. Where do you want to go?"

To bed with you for phenomenal, mind-blowing makeup sex. To an alley where I can rip open your shirt, pop your taut, hard nipples in my mouth, and then drop to my knees, delight in your underwear-melting yumminess, and suck you dry. You in me, pounding my ass like a jackhammer.

Brighton collected himself before replying. "I have a dozen errands, from website designing to car shopping."

"Car shopping? That's no small task." He shaded his eyes from the sun. "I thought yours was being repaired."

"That's before the mechanic proclaimed that I need an engine rebuild. They're never really the same after, and it costs almost as much as a new car. My warranty's been fucked."

"Why?"

Brighton shook his head and sighed. "Long story."

"I got time."

"Rogue roommate." He smirked without humor. "I won it, you know. My fraternity hosted a charity swap at Diamond Isle Casino, and they donated a Corvette as the grand prize. I had a midterm and wasn't even going to go, but Dylan kept pushing me to. It was a five-hundred-dollar donation fee, but free for frat members and a hundred dollars for their plus one. Dylan didn't have the money, so I agreed to pay it. But the evening before the party, I had a lab fee crop up—the materials needed for my chemistry midterm, which was worth half my final grade. Dylan got madder than a wet hen for not being able to go, said he didn't understand why I couldn't have waited to pay the fees and that he would've paid them when his parents sent him money. And I probably would have for anyone else, but he's always late with the rent. He accused me of reneging on a promise."

"He's not your responsibility."

"I know, but I felt guilty. I told him I wouldn't go, either, but my party chair had assigned me to help with setup. When I got there, I thought it would be fun to play a couple of hands of blackjack. Next thing I know, I'm at the slots, poker, and roulette table, downing free drinks. Then I won the car."

"Guilt is useless."

Brighton let out a soft sigh. "But that's not the worst of it. I got pretty wasted, and a guy who worked in the bistro where Dylan and I bought coffee each morning gave me a ride home. Dylan had been flirting with him for months. I thought the guy wasn't gay. Turned out he just wasn't into Dylan."

Gatien's brows scrunched. "Let me guess who he was into."

"Dylan opened the door right as the guy decided to pin me against the rail and chew half my face off. Talk about a microwaved soup sandwich. All that drama and the kiss didn't amount to a mound of pinto beans—sloppy and all over the place. His tongue plowed up my nostril like a Roto-Rooter service technician, for crying out loud."

"Was that your first kiss?"

"Don't be daft." Brighton attempted to look chagrinned with a mock glare, then flashed a sheepish grin. "Second. My first was when I was fifteen, with the son of one of my father's clients under the mistletoe at a Christmas party. Well, we thought it was mistletoe. Turned out to be poison oak, which explained the burning sensation that he claimed was nervous passion."

"Well, he sounds left of center, if you ask me. What happened with that doozy?"

"When my parents found out, my father dropped the client. Of course, my father denied our kissing being the cause, but he couldn't afford to dismiss clients for the trivial reason he gave."

"So your parents don't accept you, and you're going to go through life as a Carthusian monk?"

"I'm not a vegetarian."

"Dominican, then. Don't get smart."

"It's too painful for them, and with everything else I've put them through...."

"Put them through? You had cancer. It's not like you intentionally started being sick or snuck out of the house after curfew."

Brighton released a slow sigh. "I just don't want to make things harder for them." He glanced at the slowing streetcar. "I better skedaddle if I want to finish my errands."

"I'll go with you."

"That's boringly domesticated, you know. Not a single teaspoon of adventure."

"You have a problem with it?"

"No," Brighton hedged.

"But?"

"Gatien, I don't want to sound creepy clingy or freakish because it's only been a week, but where are things going between us? I mean, we're teammates. Do you really want to mix business with pleasure?"

"Don't you think we've already done that?"

"Yes, but you don't need to feel obligated. Besides, if you're with me—out in the open—won't people make the connection between you and Harper?"

"Why? You thought I was bi. Why wouldn't others?"

"True."

"I don't care what others think." He sighed heavily. "Listen, Brighton, I thought I made all of this clear. I want to be with you, but I have no intention of hiding. I'm not interested in someone who wants to pretend I don't exist."

The tentative quality of Gatien's voice threatened to dissolve Brighton's heart, and his own voice momentarily stuck in his throat.

"I've never been ashamed of or denied being gay. I've just never fifth-based it... until now."

He glanced at the approaching streetcar and waited for it to come to a stop. The two boarded and swiped their Jazzy Passes before moving to a middle car. All the seats were taken, so they stood in the aisle, clutching a metal pole.

"I have no intention of hiding it, either," Brighton stated as he interlaced the fingers of his free hand with Gatien's. "I'm all in."

The End

ABOUT THE AUTHOR

Thanks for reading *Defending the Net* I do hope you enjoyed Brighton and Gatien's story. I appreciate your help in spreading the word, including telling a friend. Before you go, it would mean so much to me if you would take a few minutes to write a review and share how you feel about my story so others may find my work. Reviews really do help readers find books. Please leave a review on your favorite book site.

Don't miss out on new releases, exclusive giveaways, and much more!

Join my newsletter:
https://genevivechambleeconnect.wordpress.com/newsletter/
Visit my website for my current booklist:
https://genevivechambleeconnect.wordpress.com/books-
and-short-stories/
Follow my blog Creole Bayou:
https://genevivechambleeconnect.wordpress.com

I'd love to hear from you directly, too.
Please feel free to email me at
genevivechamblee@outlook.com

Or check out my website:

https://genevivechambleeconnect.wordpress.com for updates.

ABOUT THE PUBLISHER

Hot Tree Publishing opened its doors in 2015 with an aspiration to bring quality fiction to the world of readers. With the initial focus on romance and a wide spread of romance subgenres, we envision opening up to alternative genres in the near future.

Firmly seated in the industry as a leading editing provider to independent authors and small publishing houses, Hot Tree Publishing is the sister company to Hot Tree Editing, founded in 2012. Having established in-house editing and promotions, plus having a well-respected market presence, Hot Tree Publishing endeavors to be a leader in bringing quality stories to the world of readers.

Interested in discovering more amazing reads brought to you by Hot Tree Publishing? Head over to the website for information:

www.hottreepublishing.com

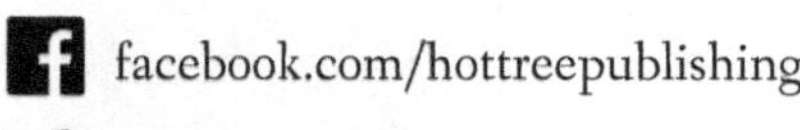

instagram.com/hottreepubs